Played!

Books by Michael A. Kahn

The Rachel Gold Mysteries
Grave Designs (The Canaan Legacy)
Death Benefits
Firm Ambitions
Due Diligence
Sheer Gall
Bearing Witness
Trophy Widow
The Flinch Factor
Face Value

The Mourning Sexton (as Michael Baron)
The Sirena Quest
Played!

Played!

A Novel

Michael A. Kahn

Poisoned Pen Press

First Edition 2017

10 9 8 7 6 5 4 3 2 1

Library of Congress Catalog Card Number: 2016961972

ISBN: 9781464208362   Trade Paperback
      9781464208379   Ebook

Poisoned Pen Press
4014 N. Goldwater Boulevard, #201
Scottsdale, Arizona 85251
www.poisonedpenpress.com
info@poisonedpenpress.com

Printed in the United States of America

For Jane, Deb, and Julie
from your brother with love and admiration

"I see great things in baseball."
—Walt Whitman

"It gets late early out there."
—Yogi Berra

Stage 1:
The Windup

Chapter One

The older members enter the traditional way, pulling up to the main entrance beneath the portico in their Mercedeses and BMWs and Cadillacs. They accept a deferential greeting from the parking valet and stroll down the main hall to the locker rooms to change into their swimwear. But others—especially the teenagers and the young mothers with children—prefer the direct route, which is through the entrance gate west of the parking lot.

On this sunny Thursday morning in late August, Patty and Josh are seated on folding chairs behind the table at the entrance gate. Patty is a freshman at Mizzou, Josh a sophomore at DePauw. Although their ostensible job is to check membership cards, this is, after all, Old Chatham Country Club, and at Old Chatham Country Club the first assignment for every summer hire is to memorize the names and faces of all members.

A mother with two small boys walks through the entrance gate.

"Good morning, Mrs. Appleton," Josh says.

"Good morning, Josh. I just saw your mother at Neiman Marcus. She told me to remind you about the Mortons' party tonight. Hello, Patty, dear."

Patty smiles. "Hi, Mrs. Appleton." She turns to the boys. "Hello, Trip. Hello, Fordham."

"Hi," the two boys respond in unison, and without enthusiasm.

As the boys follow their mother into the pool area, Patty opens her book again.

After a few minutes, Josh announces, "Oh, yeah!"

Patty turns toward him with a frown. "What?"

Grinning, he nods toward the parking lot. "The goddess has arrived."

Patty follows his gaze and then rolls her eyes. "I cannot believe you guys."

A fiery red Corvette has pulled into a parking spot two rows back from the entrance gate. The driver's door opens and a stunning blonde emerges. Today she has on a short white caftan cover-up tied loosely at the waist over a white one-piece swimsuit. She's wearing red espadrille wedge sandals and big sunglasses.

"I'm in love," Josh says.

"Forget it, you doofus." Patty shakes her head. "Look at her ring finger. And she's probably thirty years old."

Cherry Pitt reaches the entrance table where Josh and Patty are seated. She pauses and turns her beach bag toward them. Her membership card dangles from the bag handle.

"Hello, Mrs. Pitt," Josh says in a sunny voice. "It certainly is a beautiful day for a dip."

"Um-hmm," Cherry says, distracted, scanning the pool area. She walks past them onto the pool deck.

"Have a nice day, Mrs. Pitt," Josh calls after her.

Josh turns in his chair and stares at Cherry's backside as she walks toward a lounge chair.

"Have a nice day, Mrs. Pitt," Patty repeats in a nerdy voice.

"I'm in love," he says.

"Have a nice day, Mrs. Pitt," she repeats, in an even nerdier voice and returns to her book.

Josh watches as Cherry slips off her caftan, her backside to him. She bends over at the waist to set down her beach bag by the chair.

He groans. "Lord have mercy."

Patty shakes her head. "Men."

Neither of them noticed the late-model black Mustang. It entered the parking lot as Cherry was walking toward the entrance gate, paused until she had entered the pool area, and then pulled into a space facing the pool area, one row behind her red Corvette. The Mustang idles there with a throaty rumble.

Cherry settles into the lounge chair and opens a magazine on her lap.

After a few minutes, the Mustang shifts into gear, backs out of the parking space, and starts down the aisle. As it heads toward the exit, the tinted window on the driver's side lowers. A smoked-down Tiparillo arcs end over end toward the asphalt and scatters sparks as it lands.

Chapter Two

Twenty miles east of Old Chatham Country Club, on an upper floor in the Metropolitan Square Building, Milton Bernstein snorts.

We are in his office, which charitably could be described as cluttered. The desk is a jumble of yellow legal pads, marked-up pages from various court papers, stacks of pleadings binders, and deposition transcripts. Documents are scattered in piles throughout the office. A dying rubber plant sags in the corner, its last three leaves a faded brownish-green.

Milton is on the telephone, the receiver pinned between his neck and shoulder, shaking his head. The Arch and the Mississippi River are visible from the office window behind him.

"That is patently absurd," he says.

Sighing in exasperation as he listens to the lawyer on the other end of the call, Milton removes his horn-rimmed glasses, leans back in his chair, holds the glasses above his head, squints at the smudged lenses, and puts them back on.

Janet Perry is seated on the chair facing Milton's desk. She is twenty-seven years old, slender, pale and—like most associates at the international law firm of Abbott & Windsor—intense. She studies notes on a yellow legal pad on her lap.

Milton stands. He is grasping the telephone receiver with one hand and jabbing at the air with the forefinger of the other. "You can assure your client that I shall make it an unforgettable deposition. By ten a.m. next Monday I plan to be charging through the rice paddies and taking no prisoners."

If you have ever practiced in a major law firm in this country, then you know Milton Bernstein. Each such law firm has at least one Milton Bernstein. Abbott & Windsor has two, and one of them is actually named Milton Bernstein. The other, in the Chicago office, is named Melvin Needlebaum.

Regardless of their actual name, all Milton Bernsteins share a basic taxonomy. They are brilliant workaholic nerds, but—and this is important—they are not passive or submissive or bashful. Milton Bernsteins are ferocious in their commitment to the law and in their advocacy on behalf of clients, often to the exasperation of their opponents. Able to quote from memory key passages from obscure cases on even more obscure points of law, they are never at a loss for words, whether in a conference room or a courtroom. Never. They may pause for a moment, blinking at you from behind the thick lenses of their glasses, but then they will deliver a full paragraph of legalese on whatever topic you happened to raise. Although they may never have played a competitive sport in high school, and would likely have been classified 4-F by the Selective Service System, they are true warriors.

As Milton shakes his head in anger, Lawrence Armstrong strolls into the office. Lawrence nods at Janet, lifts a stack of pleading files off the chair next to hers, and sits. Lawrence Armstrong is a senior partner at Abbott & Windsor, a litigator who specializes in complex commercial disputes. Despite the salt-and-pepper comb-over, he has the handsome features of an aging Hollywood star with the build of a man who still plays tennis four mornings a week at his country club, squash racquets in the winter.

Milton is rapping a pencil on top of the computer screen. Now he jerks forward, eyebrows raised.

"Spare me, Joel," he says. "Anyone with the brains God gave a goose would know that was patently absurd."

Janet turns to Armstrong and whispers, "Are you here on the Pitt case?"

Armstrong smiles at Janet and nods. Once a noted trial lawyer, Armstrong spends most of his time these days overseeing the litigation needs of his clients. With a book of business in the mid-seven-figures, there is plenty to oversee, including the Pitt case he assigned to Milton.

Although Milton Bernstein matches no one's image of a trial lawyer, Lawrence Armstrong can see beyond that. He knows that Milton's special traits—dogged persistence, encyclopedic knowledge of the law, obsessive attention to detail—make him a good choice for the Pitt lawsuit. Indeed, those very traits, coupled with Milton's 2,800-plus billable hours per year, convinced the firm's partners, including Lawrence Armstrong, to elevate him to partnership last year, just two weeks before his thirtieth birthday. Non-equity, of course, but a partnership nevertheless.

A beep from the computer snaps Milton's head back toward the screen. As he lowers himself into his chair, he shouts into the phone, "You, sir, have launched the first missile. Prepare for Armageddon!"

He slams down the receiver and leans forward to squint at the monitor screen, reading the Westlaw search results. "Superb."

He rapidly types in a new search request, hits SEND, and then looks up, squinting first at Janet and then at Armstrong.

"Yes?"

Armstrong says, "Leonard Pitt and Associates."

Milton grins. "America's favorite chaser. Defender of the lumpen proletariat. And a genuine sleaze bag."

"Do we have a lawsuit?" Armstrong asks.

Milton rubs his hands together and raises his eyebrows. "We're getting close. Ms. Perry has been researching some of the legal issues." He turns to Janet. "Did you find the Edwards Electric case?"

Janet nods as she flips through her notes. "It seems right on point on the enterprise element." She turns to Armstrong. "To bring suit against Leonard Pitt under RICO, we need to—"

"Wait." Milton cranes his neck toward the ceiling, eyes shut tight. "Wait, wait. I think I have a better case. A 2002 decision out of the Tenth Circuit. Let's see, let's see. Ah, yes. Ames Financial Group versus toward... versus toward... aha, versus Patterson Industries, Inc. While not directly on point, there is a section on—"

"—time out." Armstrong has formed a T with his hands. "Let's cut to the chase, Milton. Where do things stand with this lawsuit?"

Milton is staring at the computer screen in disbelief. "Two hundred and eleven cases? What kind of computer search is that?"

"Milton." Armstrong's voice carries both his irritation and his authority.

Milton looks up with a sheepish grin. "Okay, okay. How much do you know about Leonard Pitt?"

"Not much," Armstrong says. "He's a politically con-nected plaintiff's personal injury lawyer."

Milton nods. "He is, indeed. By way of background, Leonard Pitt is an ex-Marine. He served in Vietnam. Started his career in municipal court, hustling the halls for clients. Remained there seven years, then he teamed up with Sam Blumenfeld. That partnership ended when Blumenfeld was convicted of eleven counts of mail fraud. He died of a stroke three years later in Marion."

"Who is she?" Janet says, taking notes.

"It," Armstrong says. "The federal penitentiary in Southern Illinois."

Milton resumes. "Pitt has been a lone wolf ever since. His firm is Leonard Pitt and Associates. The so-called 'Associates' are two third-rate lawyers, four paralegals, and somewhere between five and nine chasers."

"What are chasers?" Janet asks.

Milton grins. "The lifeblood of a personal injury lawyer's practice, Ms. Perry. They spend their days prowling the highways of metropolitan St. Louis with police radios in their cars. It's a never ending search for prospective clients of Leonard Pitt & Associates. They find them at the hospitals and even at the scenes of the accidents. They bring them in—for a handsome fee, of course."

"Isn't that illegal?" Janet asks.

"Of course it's illegal," Milton says. "Indeed, it is grounds for disbarment. More precisely, it violates Section 2-103(d) of the Code of Professional Responsibility, which provides, in pertinent part—"

"The lawsuit, Milton," Armstrong says, clearly annoyed now. "Focus, for chrissake. Tell me about the damn lawsuit."

"Ah, yes. As I was stating, the clients of Pitt's firm are semi-literate blacks and Hispanics, brought to the firm by chasers, usually within an hour or so of the traffic accident that has given rise to their sudden allure as potential clients. Pitt's paralegals get the victims to sign a fee agreement, pursuant to which the client agrees to pay Pitt forty percent of any recovery. Then they send the client to Dr. Rafael Hernandez up on the North Side. The good doctor runs up the medical expenses, which become the basis for the lawsuit that one of Pitt's underlings files on the new client's behalf. About two years later, Pitt settles the case for, say, twenty grand, takes his forty percent off the top, pays court costs, pays the good doctor, and gives the client whatever scraps are left."

Janet looks up from her notes with a frown. "But forty percent of the settlement is just eight thousand dollars. How does he make a living?"

"Volume, Ms. Perry. Leonard Pitt is the Earl Scheib of litigation. Assume his average take per case is six grand. Multiply that by four hundred, which is the number of cases he settles every year, subtract his over-head, subtract cash he pays the chasers, and he still clears well over a million dollars."

"Pitt," Armstrong says, leaning back in his chair with a frown. "Wasn't he involved in a shooting a few years back?"

"He was, indeed," Milton says. "He shot and killed an armed intruder in his living room at two in the morning. A head shot. Pitt is a gun nut. His cronies on the police force let him practice on their target range. He's a big-game hunter. Heads west each fall, usually to Wyoming, for the elk season. Been on several African safaris. I understand that the walls of his law firm's reception area are decorated with the heads of animals he's killed.

"Is he married?" Janet asks.

Milton smiles. "For the third time. Wife number one was the former Evelyn Palermo. They were married for sixteen years. Two daughters. Divorced twelve years ago. Married wife number two a year later. That one lasted three years. No children. His third wife is his former secretary, Mary Charissa Kochilinski. She shortened her name to Cherry Koke after high school. She worked at the Kmart in Festus before she took a job with Pitt. However, she is not just another pretty bimbo. My investigator says she is one tough lady. Very smart, very crafty. Pitt had her handle the payoffs to the chasers. That is a job that takes more than a little grit."

"How old is wife number three?" Armstrong asks.

"Thirty-one," Milton says. "They've been married three years. No children. She had a miscarriage a few months after they got married. According to my investigator, she was pregnant when they got married."

"They're still married?" Janet asks.

"Oh, yes. Probably for the duration. Leonard became a Roman Catholic between his second and third wives. He's a big pal of the Archbishop. Goes to mass each Sunday. As you well know, the Catholic Church does not look kindly on divorce."

"So where does our client fit in?" Armstrong asks.

"Mid-Continent Casualty is the third-largest insurer of automobiles in metropolitan St. Louis. It settles seventy to a hundred of Leonard Pitt's fender-benders a year. Comes to about five hundred thousand dollars annually. They think Pitt has defrauded them out of more than two million dollars over the last ten years."

"What about the criminal authorities?" Armstrong asks.

"They tried. The U.S. Attorney wasn't interested. The state prosecutor seemed interested at first, but that investigation fizzled out under mysterious circumstances."

Janet asks, "What kind of mysterious circumstances?"

Milton smiles. "Let's just say that the influence Leonard Pitt wields within the state judicial system is not insubstantial."

"What do you have so far?" Armstrong asks.

"Ah, yes." Milton gives him a smile that looks more like a grimace. He turns toward his credenza, sorts through a pile of documents, pulls out two, and spins back toward Armstrong and Janet with the documents held high.

"Ladies and gentlemen," he announces, "I present the smoking guns. Plaintiff's Exhibits One and Two."

Chapter Three

Hal is a devotee of Mrs. Pitt's derriere. From his perch on the lifeguard stand he has admired it since she began coming to the pool three weeks ago. Not that the rest of her isn't awesome. Her perky boobs are sexy, her dancer's legs are hot, and the occasional hint of a camel toe, especially when she comes out of the water, has become a staple of his masturbation fantasies.

But her tush is to die for. Especially in the white one-piece she's wearing today. He loves the way it cups those round cheeks as she walks across the deck, the way the bottom rides up as she swims her laps so that when she climbs the ladder to the deck she pauses to reach back and snap the bottom back in place. Moments like that make him glad he is wearing his orange lifeguard swim trunks over his snug red Speedo.

"Hal?"

He looks down.

Gina is at the foot of the lifeguard platform gazing up at him. She points to her wristwatch. "Break time."

"Dude."

He climbs down and stands facing the water as Gina climbs up the ladder.

"Okay," she says.

He nods, staring at the water. The Old Chatham pool is huge, with four lifeguard stands at twelve, three, six, and nine on the clock. Cherry is out there now, in the adult section near the center of the pool. She is on her back on an inflatable blue raft.

Decision time.

Hal has given this moment, this opportunity, a great deal of thought since Mrs. Pitt began coming to the pool on Tuesdays and Thursdays. The lounge chair option seems too intrusive, since she's usually reading a book or talking on her cell phone. And her lap sessions aren't an option. People swimming laps don't talk. But these raft times—well, no book, no phone.

Go for it.

Hal slides off his lifeguard trunks, sets his aviator sunglasses on top of them, dives into the water, and swims toward her raft.

"Hey, Mrs. Pitt."

She turns her head toward him.

He smiles. "You're not going to believe this."

She stares at him.

"One of the girls in the *Sports Illustrated* swimsuit issue, the one last February—she had on the same swimsuit you're wearing, and you look even better than she did."

She stares at him.

Hal forces a bigger smile.

After a moment, she says, "You're right."

"You saw the issue?"

"No."

Hal frowns. "Huh?"

"You said I wouldn't believe it. I don't."

She starts to turn away.

"Wait. How 'bout this? Sit on my face and I'll guess your weight."

She lowers her sunglasses and stares at him, unsmiling. "You'd drown."

Hal gives her a lame smile. "I can float."

She puts her sunglasses back in place. "So can Ivory Soap."

She paddles away from him toward the far side of the pool.

Hal watches her for a moment and then shakes his head. "Nicely played, schmuck."

Chapter Four

Milton hands one of the documents to Armstrong. "This is Exhibit One."

Armstrong studies it. "A check for eighteen thousand dollars."

He tilts it toward Janet so that she can see.

"Payable to Manuel Ortega and Leonard Pitt & Associates," he reads.

"You are correct, sir. You will note that it is drawn on the account of Mid-Continent Casualty Insurance Company. The memo line indicates that it is in settlement of Mr. Ortega's lawsuit against one Ralph Cantwell, whom Mid-Continent insured."

Armstrong looks up. "Okay?"

"And now—" Milton presents the other document to Janet. "—I present Exhibit Two."

Armstrong comes around behind Janet so that he can see the document as well:

LEONARD PITT & ASSOCIATES
CLOSING STATEMENT

Client: Manuel Ortega

Settlement Payment:		$13,000.00
		LESS:
Attorney Fee (40%):		5,200.00
Court Costs:		225.00
Medical Bills:		2,225.00
NET TO CLIENT:		$5,250.00
Date:	March 20, 2009	
Accepted:	Manuel Ortega	

Armstrong looks up at Milton. "And the punch line?"

Milton leans forward, his eyes bright behind the thick lenses. "Ortega received that closing statement from Pitt when he came in to pick up his settlement money. It states that the case settled for thirteen grand! But the sole check Mid-Continent ever issued in settlement of that case is the one I just handed you."

Armstrong looks down at the copy of the eighteen-thousand-dollar check and then at the closing statement in Janet's hand. He raises his eyes toward Milton and nods.

Milton leans back, grinning. "Not bad, eh? We find a couple more like that and we've got old Leonard Pitt by the short hairs! Short hairs? Hmmm. What a superb idea."

Milton lurches forward and starts typing a search request into the computer.

"I don't get it," Janet says.

"If this is part of pattern" Armstrong explains, "then Leonard Pitt is defrauding his clients *and* the insurance company. He settles this case with the insurance company for eighteen thousand dollars. They issue him a check for eighteen thousand. Then he calls his client and tells him the great news: he was able to settle the case for *thirteen* thousand. The kind of people Pitt represents—to them the whole legal system is an intimidating mystery. They're happy to get any money, especially after they've waited so long. If Pitt tells them that thirteen thousand is a good settlement, they'll believe him."

Milton looks up from the computer. "Precisely! The insurance company gets screwed out of the extra five grand, the client gets screwed out of his share of the two grand, and Pitt pockets it all."

Janet mulls that over. "So if Pitt settles one hundred cases a year with our client and skims that kind of money out of each settlement—" She frowns as she tries to do the calculation in her head."

Milton says, "You're talking a half million, Ms. Perry. That's fraud with a capital F. And if my investigators come up with two more witnesses like Mr. Ortega, we are going to have Leonard Pitt right—"

The computer BEEPS.

Milton leans forward to squint at the screen and then lurches back with a groan. "Another Posner opinion? Lord have mercy!"

Chapter Five

Hal steps out of the bathroom, pauses to check his reflection in the hall mirror, points an index finger at that reflection, winks, and then walks down the hall to the den, where his older brother is frowning as he taps out an e-mail on his iPhone.

"Like I was saying," Hal says, "it's simple. A summer of sun and romance on the pool deck at Old Chatham. What could beat that?"

Milton looks up from his iPhone, looks down again, presses SEND, looks up, and shrugs. "I suppose that sounds better than three months in a warehouse reviewing documents."

Hal grins. "I sure hope so, Bro. This is my last chance. I'm getting old. Next summer I'll be stuck in that warehouse or doing whatever the heck it is that paralegals do. Stuck in some law office staring out a window that doesn't open. Wearing a suit and lugging a briefcase." He shakes his head. "For the rest of my life. Jeez."

"Are you head lifeguard?"

"For another week or so. When the outdoor pool closes for the season, they'll have me working the indoor pool. But for now, I'm on outdoor duty."

"How is it?"

"Not bad. There must be a dozen mommies at the pool each day. Sometimes more. Some are real foxes, too. Way I figure, most of them are married to big-shot bankers and MBAs and corporate lawyers. You know the type. Guys just like you, Bro. Twelve hours a day, six days a week, lots of travel. Just think of those poor women. Stuck at home with the kids all day, climbing the walls, maybe looking for a little excitement."

Milton raises his eyebrows. "Have you identified any prospects?"

"A few. It's just like the song."

"What song?"

Hal hums a few bars from Wilbert Harrison's "Kansas City."

Hal gives his older brother a wink. "They got some pretty little women there and I'm going to get me some."

"Crazy, not pretty."

Hal turns to see Peggy Bernstein standing in the doorway.

"Crazy?" Hal repeats.

Peggy nods. "Not pretty little women, you bozo. Crazy little women. That's how the song goes. *Crazy* little women."

"Oh, yeah." Hal grins. "Crazy. Right. Crazier the better."

Peggy shakes her head. "You're not referring to those poor young mothers at Old Chatham Country Club, are you? Or rather, those rich young mothers?"

Hal shrugs. "I'm just trying to bring a ray of sunshine into their lives, Peggy."

Peggy places her hand over her heart. "I am deeply moved by your *noblesse oblige*." She turns to Milton. "The girls are upstairs waiting for a goodnight kiss from their daddy.

Hal and Milton get up together.

"Gotta go," Hal says.

"Oh?" Milton says.

Hal shrugs. "Lost a hundred forty dollars in a poker game last night. Guy drew an inside straight on the last hand. Gotta get back there tonight and win some back."

He turns to Peggy. "Thanks for dinner, Sis. It was totally super."

Peggy smiles and shakes her head. "Next time I'll fix you a bucket of oysters, Stud. We have to keep you in shape for all those mommies."

Hal laughs. "Sounds good, Dr. Peg."

He leans over and gives her kiss. "See ya, kiddo."

"Thanks for those beautiful flowers," she says. "And the girls loved those princess outfits. You're a wonderful uncle, Harold."

He shrugs. "That's 'cause they're wonderful nieces."

She watches her husband and his younger brother walk to the front door, where Hal gives Milton a playful punch on the shoulder. Peggy marvels again at how those two could be siblings. While Milton's bloodline looks as if it traces directly back to the butcher or rebbe in a nineteenth-century Russian shtetl, Hal's appearance suggests a DNA link to some Cossack marauder who inserted himself, literally, into the Bernstein bloodline. Hal stands a head taller than Milton. Hal has straight blond hair, chiseled features, blue eyes, and a jock's build, while his older brother has kinky black hair, a bulbous nose, thick glasses, and a body type that even Peggy had to admit could sympathetically be described as solid.

But love is mysterious. Peggy's girlfriends unanimously agree that Hal is a hunk, and by the *People Magazine* standards for Sexiest Man, he certainly is. But not for Peggy. She's had the hots for Milton since that first day in chem lab freshman year at M.I.T., when they were paired as lab partners. She dragged him back to her dorm room after their fifth lab session and seduced him right there. And even now, twelve years later and twenty pounds heavier than that first time on that dorm-room bed, she still has the hots for Milton and, by all signs, he still has the hots for her.

• • ● • •

Having kissed his daughters goodnight and tucked them into bed, Milton bends at the landing to scoop up Cleo the cat. He sets the cat down at the bottom of the stairs and pauses at the entrance to the kitchen. Peggy is washing the dishes with her back to him.

Milton smiles as he approaches her. He hugs her from behind.

"Excellent dinner," he says

Peggy looks back at him. "Thanks, sweetie."

Milton takes a dish towel and starts drying dishes.

Peggy says, "I feel bad for your little brother."

"Sounds to me like he's having a satisfactory experience. I can think of worse jobs."

"It's a job for a high school kid, Milton. Your brother is almost twenty-four. He couldn't get into law school, so now he's going to get a paralegal degree." She shakes her head. "He's always been in your shadow."

"Not in my family."

"Your mom is an idiot. Same with your aunts and your uncle."

"They worship him. Everyone did. Even my grand-mothers."

Peggy shakes her head. "For no reason."

"He certainly was a better baseball player than me."

"Big deal."

"He was a big deal, Peggy. Remember, he was the only guy from St. Louis named a *Parade Magazine* High School Baseball All-American. That article said his pitches were as accurate as an Army Ranger sharpshooter."

"Then he should have enlisted."

Milton sighs. "I'll always feel bad for my dad. He loved baseball so much. He'd have been so proud of Hal. He never even got to see him pitch in high school."

Milton picks up a pot from the rack and starts drying it. "Hal may not have been the brightest kid in class, Peggy, but he was a remarkable pitcher. I used to catch for him in the backyard after Dad died. Hal was still little back then. Maybe ten, eleven. Even so, he could hit any target I gave him. Heck, I was such a klutz it was even a challenge for me to get the ball back to him on the fly, and I was in high school. The kid was amazing. That arm earned him a full ride to Mizzou."

"And how long did that last?" She shakes her head. "His career ends before his junior year with that motor-cycle accident."

"Most people never get that far."

"Most people aren't your brother, Milton. He's put himself in a no-win situation. It's sad, I'll admit. He'll always compare himself to you. He'll be lucky to land a job with some sleazy personal injury firm."

"He could make a career out of it."

"That's not my point. Look at you. Law degree with honors from University of Chicago, clerkship with a federal judge, now a partner in a big law firm."

"Non-equity partner."

"Doesn't matter. Your little brother could never compete with that. He should have done something else. He'd be a great high school coach. Or he could go into sales. Everyone loves the guy. He could sell ice to Eskimos. But he's not you, and he shouldn't try to be."

"He'll do fine. He might surprise you."

Peggy looks over at him and raises her eyebrows. "That's what I'm worried about."

Milton smiles. "Meanwhile, he'll have a unique summer."

Milton puts down the dish towel and takes Peggy in his arms. "He told me some of those country club mothers are real foxes."

Peggy rolls her eyes. "Oh he did, did he?"

"He said they aren't teeny boppers but mature women."

"Oh, really?"

"Guess what else he told me?"

"I can't even imagine."

"He said they lose all their inhibitions after going through labor."

"Oh, my."

Milton gives her a kiss on the nose. "Do you think that's true?"

Peggy tries to look serious. "That sounds like an untested hypothesis."

"Maybe we should test it. After all, you were the chemistry major. Isn't that what you scientists do?"

She raises her eyebrows. "My laboratory is upstairs."

"Excellent."

As Milton leads her out of the kitchen toward the stairs, Peggy laughs and says, "Isn't science wonderful?"

Chapter Six

Primo Dog Tuesday.

That's Hal's name for it. During the year he worked as a fitness trainer at the East Bank Club in Chicago he became addicted to Chicago-style hot dogs—those Vienna Beef marvels on poppy seed buns with yellow mustard, neon relish, and green sport peppers. When he moved back to St. Louis, he scouted out places to satisfy that passion, and Primo Dog was one that made the cut. Although Woofies is still Hal's numero uno in St. Louis, Primo Dog is the closest one to Old Chatham Country Club, and that's where Hal heads at twelve-fifteen each Tuesday on his lunch break.

Primo Dog Tuesday.

Ray mans the grill. He nods as Hal walks up to the counter. "The usual, big guy?"

"You got it, dude."

A few minutes later, the tray of food in hand, Hal uses his foot to push open the screen door to the tables outside. That's when he sees her. He stares, and the door swings back against him. Seated alone at a table facing him is Mrs. Pitt. She's wearing skinny jeans, a red tank top, and sunglasses.

"Mind if I join you?" he asks.

Hal waits for her answer. She is holding the hot dog—not the bun, just the dog—between her thumb and forefinger. Long nails, red polish. She glances up, shrugs as if to say *suit yourself*, and bites off the end of the hot dog.

With a nervous smile, Hal sits down. He unwraps his hot dog and takes a big bite.

"Didn't see you at the pool today," he says as he chews.

"That's because I wasn't here."

"Yeah." He forces a laugh. "Guess that's probably why."

He takes another bite of his hot dog as he tries to think of something to say. He's usually pretty good with chicks, but with this one he's in brain freeze.

Finally, he says, "I read somewhere that hot dogs are bad for you."

She looks at him from behind her sunglasses but says nothing.

"Too many nitrates." Hal shrugs. "They say you shouldn't eat them."

Mrs. Pitt studies him as she bites off another piece of the hot dog and slowly chews it. "What do you suggest I eat instead?"

"Don't know." He shrugs. "Guess I'm a big one to talk."

"Are you?"

He tries to grin, completely lost now, treading water.

"I'm married," she says.

"Oh. I'm not."

She lowers her head to stare at him over her sunglasses. "How long is your break?"

Hal checks his watch. "I've got to head back in ten minutes."

"Too bad." She stands. "See you around."

"Wait." Hal stumbles to his feet. "How about tomorrow? It's one of my days off. Wednesdays and Thursdays."

Mrs. Pitt pauses, staring at him from behind her sunglasses. "How about what tomorrow?"

Hal tries another grin. "Whatever takes longer than ten minutes, I guess."

She glances down at his empty plate. "Does anything take you longer than thirty seconds?"

"Depends what you have in mind."

"A beer."

"Sure. I can make that last longer than ten minutes. Guaranteed."

She smiles. "That sounds nice." She tells him her address. "Come in through the alley. Twelve-fifteen."

Stunned, Hal watches her walk toward her Corvette, staring at that awesome little round butt swinging back and forth in the tight jeans. He jogs over to her car as she starts to gun the engine."

"Mrs. Pitt, I don't even know your first name."

"Cherry."

She guns the engine again, puts it into gear, and roars away.

Hal watches her speed down the street.

"Cherry," he repeats aloud, and then he smiles. "Dude."

Watching her red Corvette disappear around the corner, he never once considers the improbability of their encounter at Primo Dog. If you'd asked him right then, if you'd come up to him as he stood out there by the curb in the warm afternoon sun and asked him if he didn't think it a bit odd that the wife of a millionaire lawyer, a woman you'd normally expect to see at

lunch at the Zodiac Room in the Neiman Marcus at
Plaza Frontenac or maybe at the Women's Exchange on
Ladue, just happened to be eating at a hot dog joint in
West County at exactly the same time as him—well, if
you would have asked him that, he would have given
you one of those thousand-watt smiles and a shrug and
said, "Hey, dude, guess the lady's got good taste."

But at the same time *as you?* you'd ask. *On the only
day of the week you go there?*

Another shrug, and then a cocky wink. "Luck of the
draw, dude. Luck of the draw."

Chapter Seven

Twenty-four hours later, we are in Cherry Pitt's kitchen. The telephone on the granite countertop starts to ring. Cherry comes in from the den and lifts the receiver.

"Yes?"

She takes a seat on the bar stool. Following behind her is Hal, a bottle of Corona in hand.

"Mrs. Pitt," says the familiar voice on the other end of the line, "this is Belinda. Mr. Pitt wanted me to call to remind you that you're supposed to meet him downtown at five-thirty for the reception at the Missouri Athletic Club.

Hal takes a seat at the breakfast room table facing Cherry.

Actually, staring at Cherry. She is wearing a St. Louis Blues jersey and sandals. The jersey ends mid-thigh. Hal is staring at those long, tanned legs.

"Okay," Cherry says into the phone. "I'll be there."

"Thank you, Mrs. Pitt. Have a nice day."

There is a click on the other end and then the sound of the dial tone. Cherry looks up at Hal for a moment, the cordless phone still against her ear. Turning her head to block Hal's view of the receiver, she presses the disconnect button, silencing the buzz.

And then she says into the phone, "But that's not fair. Jesus. Leonard."

She parts her legs slightly, revealing the thin strip of her white cotton panties.

"Come on, Leonard. I can't believe you."

As she pretends to listen, she squirms on the chair, and her legs open and close.

Hal is mesmerized.

Cherry stares down at the floor, slowly shaking her head. "Can't this wait 'til tomorrow?" she says into the phone.

A pause.

A sigh.

Legs part again.

"All right," she says. "I said *all right*. Where are they located? Wait a minute."

As she reaches across for a notepad and paper, her legs open wide. Hal chokes on his beer.

"Okay. One-thirty? Is that north of the Old Post Office? Okay. I'll try to be there. Okay, Leonard. I'll do it."

She hangs up, her head slumped. She sighs. She closes her legs.

Hal says, "Problem?"

Cherry looks up, dejected. "That was my husband. The bastard claims I'm spending too much money. He just told me he canceled my credit cards and put me on an allowance. An allowance? Have you ever? I have to go downtown to meet with his accountants."

"Oh, man. Bummer."

Cherry stands up. "I need to change. I have to leave here in ten minutes. I'm sorry, Hal. Maybe some other time, huh?"

Hal struggles to his feet, covering the crotch of his shorts with the beer bottle. "Sure. No problem. I hope you get it worked out."

She stops him as he walks past her toward the back door. "It was so nice to be able to spend time with you. You're such a sweet man, Hal. We'll find another time later."

"Sure. That'd be awesome."

"Leave the beer bottle here. I'll throw it out."

He sets it down.

She smiles, grabs him gently by the crotch, and widens her eyes. "Oh, my. Nice."

With her other hand, she pulls his face down to hers and gives him a kiss.

After Hal leaves, she puts on a rubber dishwashing glove, picks up his empty beer bottle by the rim, and carefully places it in the back of the cabinet below the sink, behind the two boxes of dishwasher detergent.

Chapter Eight

We are in the small kitchen in a run-down third-floor apartment on Miami Street in the section of St. Louis known as South City. Milton Bernstein is seated at the round table across from Gloria Sanchez, a heavyset Hispanic woman in her fifties. Seated next to Milton is Janet Perry. She's scribbling notes on her yellow legal pad as Milton studies the document Ms. Sanchez has just handed him.

"I see." Milton nods his head. "And this document is what Mr. Pitt gave you when you came to his office for your settlement money?"

"*Si.* He give this to me. He say I need to sign in order for to give to me my money."

Milton points at one of the line items on the statement. "It says here that his law firm settled your case for eleven thousand dollars. Is that what he told you, Mrs. Sanchez?"

"That what he say. He tell me sign right there—" she leans forward to point to her signature "—and then he give to me the money for my share."

"Did he say anything about the settlement? Did he tell you it was a good settlement?"

"*Si*. He tell me insurance company only want to pay seven thousand dollars but that he talk and talk and bang table and talk more and finally they say *si* to eleven. He tell me if I don't sign right then, the insurance might go right back down to seven.

Milton glances over at Janet and nods, barely able to restrain his smile. He turns back to Mrs. Sanchez. "Did Mr. Pitt ever show you the check that the insurance company sent him to settle your case?"

"No, *Señor*. He say he pay me direct and he worry about getting that check to be cashed."

"And did he pay you your share of the settlement?"

Gloria Sanchez smiles and nods. "*Si, Señor.*"

"According to this statement you signed, you were to receive 5,820 dollars."

"*Si, Señor*. He had his assistant to give to me the money."

"In cash?"

Gloria smiles. "*Si, Señor.*"

• • ● • •

Ten minutes later, on the sidewalk outside the apartment building, Milton turns to Janet with a manic grin.

"Sanchez makes three, Ms. Perry, and three is our magic number. We definitely have a lawsuit. I will notify Mr. Armstrong when we return to the office and he will notify the client. You need to contact our process server. Tell him we should have our lawsuit on file and ready to serve by the beginning of next week."

"Okay."

"Ah, Ms. Perry." Milton laughs. "We are about to ruin Leonard Pitt's summer. And, let's hope, many summers to come."

Chapter Nine

Another crash of thunder. The rain pelts Hal's bedroom window. He's on his bed, head propped on a pillow, watching the Cardinals game on TV, sipping a Bud Light. He's wearing nothing but a pair of Voltron boxer shorts—the one with the image of the Power Sword.

Another crash of thunder, this one sounding closer. A miserable night out there. Perfect weather at the ballgame, though. Cards are playing the Padres.

Southern California. Rain. What was that song?

Oh, yeah. "It Never Rains In Southern California." He hums the tune, recalling the lyrics.

It never rains in California,
But girl, don't they warn ya,
It pours, man, it pours.

Spent six months out there last year, mainly working the counter at that In-N-Out Burger in Glendale. Just like the guy in the song—hoping to land something in TV or the movies. And just like the guy in the song—ended up out of work, out of bread, underloved, underfed, wanting to go home.

Hal tilts his head and frowns, listening. A faint chime of the doorbell to his apartment. He sits up, grabs a pair of shorts, steps into them, and zips and buttons them as he walks to the front hall.

"Who is it?" he says.

"Open up, Hal. It's me."

Cherry Pitt? What the heck?

He unlocks and opens the door.

Cherry. Standing there in a stylish black raincoat, an overnight bag in one hand, car keys in the other.

She smiles. "Can I come in?"

"Uh, sure."

She walks past him into the small living room, tosses the overnight bag onto the couch, and turns to him.

He says, "What's up?

"My husband left town today. He won't be back until tomorrow night."

Hal looks at her uncertainly, not yet ready to believe his luck. "Oh?"

Cherry unbuckles her raincoat. "I'm all wet."

She lets the raincoat drop to the floor and turns sideways as she shakes out her hair. Hal stares. She's wearing nothing but black thong panties and black pumps.

"Is that the bedroom?" she asks, nodding toward it.

"Uh, yeah."

She glances back with a smile as she sashays toward the bedroom.

An hour later, Cherry comes out of the bedroom, naked. In the darkened living room, she kneels down by the couch, where there are dozens of magazines in piles. She opens one—a *Sports Illustrated*—flips through it, tears out a page, turns a few more, tears out another page, closes it, sets it down on the couch, reaches for another one. Within a few minutes she has maybe two dozen pages in a pile on the couch to her left and seven magazines scattered on the couch to her right. She gathers the seven magazines, crouches down low in front of the couch, and slides them far underneath. Then she reaches for her overnight bag, unzips it, and stuffs the loose pages into it.

"Cherry?"

She turns as she slowly zips up her bag. Hal is standing in the doorway.

"What are you doing, babe?" he asks.

She walks over to him and kisses him on the neck.

In a husky voice, she says, "I was looking for my toothpaste."

She pushes him backward back into the bedroom and onto the bed, crawling on top of him.

Between kisses, she says, "I thought you were asleep."

"I was. I'm up now."

She moves her face slowly down his chest and stomach. "Ah, I see everyone is up."

And she lowers her head.

"Oh, my God."

Twenty minutes later, Cherry is in the bathroom rinsing her mouth. She leans back to peer into the bedroom just as it's illuminated by a flash of lightning. Hal is on his back, snoring.

She dries her mouth on a towel and walks back into the bedroom. Stopping by the window, she turns to gaze down at Hal as the distant thunder rumbles. She steps away from the window and slides into bed.

Barely visible through that window, down on the one-way street below, parked in front of the apartment building, is that same late-model black Mustang last seen on the country club parking lot. Although the rain has stopped, another bolt of lightning flashes far off. The driver's window is rolled down, an arm resting on the window. There is a dim reddish flare of light near the hand. The lighted tip of a Tiparillo. The hand disappears into the car for a moment, reappears, and drops the cigar out the window. It lands on the grass near two other Tiparillo butts.

• ● ● ● •

"So divorce him," Hal says.

It's the next morning. Hal and Cherry are in the kitchen. Hal is eating a bowl of Cheerios. Cherry sips her cup of coffee.

"It's not that easy," she says.

"Sure it is. No kids, no custody battles."

"And no money."

Hal frowns. "No money? With that house? What's your old man do for a living?"

"He's a lawyer downtown."

"So's my brother. Lawyers make a good living." He pauses, eyebrows raised. "Holy mackerel, are you married to Leonard Pitt?"

She nods.

"That dude must be loaded. I've seen his TV commercials. Damn, Cherry, if you hate him, divorce him. You're probably entitled to half his money. Jeez, I should have thought of that before."

"Leonard already did."

"Huh?"

"Before we got married he made me sign one of

those prenups. Last month I showed it to a lawyer. He says it's airtight."

"What's it say?"

"I waive all rights to Leonard's property. If we get divorced, I get an alimony payment of one thousand dollars a month for two years."

"That's peanuts."

"It gets worse. If we stay married but he dies before me, I get a total property settlement equal to one thousand dollars a month for however many months we were married beyond two years. We've been married four years and three months. If he died tomorrow, I'd get twenty-seven thousand dollars. Period.

"That totally sucks. What a creep."

Cherry reaches for his hand. "I hate him, Hal. If I had enough money, I'd walk out on him today."

"We don't need any money, Cherry. We've got each other."

She comes around the table and sits on his lap.

"My savior," she coos.

Chapter Ten

Cherry Pitt is seated at her makeup desk in the guest bedroom, two doors down the hall from the master bedroom. Wearing disposable latex gloves, she carefully cuts the word "Friday" out of a page torn from a magazine. She has her cell phone cradled against her neck as she cuts.

Hal answers on the third ring. "Cherry?"

"Hey, Stud. You still coming tomorrow?"

Hal chuckles. "I'm hoping at least twice."

"Promises, promises."

"I miss you, babe."

"I miss you, too. Can you do me a favor?"

She daubs the cut-out word with glue and presses it into place on the sheet of paper in front of her.

"Sure," Hal says. "You name it."

"Is there a Walgreens or CVS near you?"

"There's a Walgreens."

"Can you stop in there on your way over tomorrow? I need a roll of duct tape."

"Duct tape? Whoa. Are we talking some kinky action?"

"Dream on, lover boy. I'll see you at twelve-fifteen."

"I'm on it. See you then."

"Oh, Hal. About the duct tape."

"Yeah?"

"Do me a favor. Don't pay cash. Put it on your credit card."

"Charge it?"

"And bring me the receipt."

"Really?"

"Please."

"Well, okay."

She takes the phone in her hand, disconnects the call, and sets it down on the table. Still wearing the gloves, she lifts up the sheet of paper to study her handiwork, nods, and goes back to work.

Thirty minutes later she's finished. Some of the words are composed of letters cut from different magazine ads. Others are entire words cut from the ads. The result is a complex jumble of fonts, colors, and sizes. But the message is straightforward:

> We have your wife. uNLeSs you WirE
> $1 miLLioN into account 113452107,
> BANquE KreDIt suISSe, geNEvA, by 11
> aM this FRIDAY, she will DIE and WE
> will eXPosE Your INSURANCE ScAm!

Still wearing the gloves, she slides the ransom note into a manila envelope, lifts the edge of the mattress, sets the envelope on the box springs, and lets the mattress drop down.

Chapter Eleven

It's almost noon.

We're in the men's room at the SharpShooters Club, just down the hall from the Safari Dining Room.

Marble sinks, polished brass fixtures, neat stacks of cotton hand towels, and a sumptuous row of porcelain urinals fit for the gods. An elegant room. Exactly what you would expect to find in the most exclusive gun club in St. Louis, founded in 1904 to coincide with the World's Fair and the Olympics, both held in St. Louis that year. Over the decades its guests—many displayed in framed photographs in the lobby—have included two Presidents, several CEOs of Fortune 500 companies, and various other celebrities from the worlds of Hollywood (that one on the far right is Clint Eastwood), music (yep, that's Ted Nugent), and sports (including several Cardinals but no longer O.J. Simpson, whose photo came down a few months before the jury verdict).

And thus we are in one of the last men's rooms in St. Louis where you would expect to find Jimmy Torrado. He combs his thick black hair in the large mirror over the marble sinks, trying to maintain his cool. He runs his finger under his collar and then straightens his tie, checking his reflection. He isn't used to wearing a coat and tie, but you do what you gotta do. Trailed the son of a bitch for three days, trying to figure out how to get close enough to do it, to get past his driver and his secretary and the rest of the damn entourage. And then it hit him, like one of those bulbs clicking on in a cartoon: serve the asshole in the crapper.

Jimmy leans forward and stares at himself in the mirror. There is a little blackhead on the bridge of his nose. Yes, sir, he says to himself as he pinches it out between his thumbnail and fingernail, you got to get up pretty early in the a.m. to get the drop on Jimmy Torrado. Fucking aye, baby.

He hears a rustle of newspaper from one of the toilet stalls. Then the sound of toilet paper unrolling.

Jimmy Torrado takes the documents out of his blue plastic briefcase and waits. The toilet flushes, the stall door opens. A silver-haired guy steps out, a *St. Louis Business Journal* folded under his arm. He moves past Jimmy toward one of the sinks like Jimmy wasn't even fucking there.

Yep, that's him.

Jimmy waits until the guy starts washing his hands. Big green gems on his cuff links, manicured fingernails, gold Rolex watch. Guy is loaded, no question.

"You Leonard Pitt?"

The silver-haired guy turns his head toward him as he lathers his hands. Doesn't say a thing. Just stares at Jimmy with those cold blue eyes. Sub-zero eyes. Rinses the suds off his hands, reaches for a towel, taking his own sweet goddamn time, drying his hands like he has all fucking day, Jimmy just standing there, shifting his weight from one foot to the other.

Still drying his hands, the guy looks at Jimmy, sizing him up.

In a raspy voice, he says, "What do you want?"

Making it sound like more of a demand than a question.

Jimmy Torrado takes a step toward him and holds out the court papers. "Mr. Leonard Pitt, you are hereby served with the summons and complaint in this here lawsuit. You're also served with a motion for preliminary injunction and, uh, some of these other court papers."

Pitt doesn't take them. Doesn't even glance at them. Just stares at Jimmy Torrado, who is starting to feel like a total douchebag standing there with the papers in his outstretched hand and this arrogant bastard still drying his fucking hands and giving him a look like Jimmy's some kind of retard.

"You gonna take 'em or what?"

After a moment, Pitt's lips curl into a smile. An arrogant smile. He turns away and drops the towel into the hamper.

He turns back toward Jimmy. "Leave the papers by the sink, greaseball, and get the fuck out of here."

Torrado slaps the papers down on the sink and grabs his plastic briefcase. He opens the door, pauses, and looks back.

"You've just been served, asshole!"

After Torrado leaves, Leonard Pitt glances down at the stack of papers. The top page is the summons in *Mid-Continent Casualty Assurance Co. v. Leonard M. Pitt.* He lifts the document. Below it is the complaint.

He skims through it, expressionless. Below that is the motion for a preliminary injunction and the supporting memorandum of law. Pitt leafs slowly through the motion, stopping at the final page:

```
Wherefore, this honorable Court
should enter a preliminary injunc-
tion freezing all liquid assets of
defendant Pitt by enjoining and pro-
hibiting defendant and any banks,
savings and loan associations, or
other financial institutions with
whom defendant Pitt or his firm main-
tains any accounts from removing,
withdrawing, or otherwise trans-
ferring any money out of any such
accounts.
```

He rereads that final paragraph. After a moment, he looks up at his reflection in the mirror, his frown fading. There is a hint of a smile as he turns away.

Chapter Twelve

At twelve-ten the following afternoon, Hal pulls his car into the alley behind the Pitt house, steps through a gap in the bushes, and bounds up to the back door. He is carrying the duct tape in one hand. He raps on the door. Cherry opens it.

Hal's grin fades. "What happened?"

Cherry is wearing dark glasses. Her face is grim. "I'm getting out of this house for good."

"Tell me."

"Come on in."

She closes the door after him, walks over to the fridge, and opens it.

"Have a beer," she says, pointing to the bottles on the top shelf. "I've already had three."

Hal reaches in, takes one, and steps back with a confused look.

"Okay," he says, and twists off the beer cap.

Cherry says, "We had a fight."

"About what?"

"I told him I wanted a divorce."

She walks toward the living room, pausing to look back at him. "Take a look."

Hal follows her, stopping at the doorway to the living room.

"Holy crap."

The room is a mess: furniture overturned, a piece of pottery in shards on the carpet, the fireplace screen jammed in the fireplace.

Hal turns to her. "What happened?"

"He went nuts."

"Your husband did all this?"

"And this."

She removes her sunglasses. She has a black eye.

"And this." She opens the top buttons of her shirt to reveal scratches on her chest.

"That bastard. I'll kill him."

"No you won't. He's a dangerous man, Hal. The people who work for him are even worse."

"Then let's call the police."

"Forget the police, Hal. I just want to get out of here. And never come back."

He reaches tenderly for her face. She flinches.

"Come with me," he says. "You can stay at my apartment."

She shakes her head. "I don't want to get you involved, honey."

"I am involved. I want to be involved. You need someone to protect you."

She reaches for his hand, her eyes watering. "Dear sweet Hal. You don't know what he's like."

"Screw him. It's you I care about."

"Not your apartment. It has to be somewhere he'd never look. Somewhere I can disappear for a while."

"Wherever it is, I'll take you there."

She smiles at him. "You shouldn't get involved, sweetheart. It's my problem."

"It's our problem, Cherry. Pack an overnight bag and let's get out of here."

She gives him a tender kiss. "My protector."

"Damn straight, girl."

• ● ● ● •

Hal is on his cell phone when Cherry comes back downstairs to the kitchen

"It's probably a virus," he says into the phone. "One of those twenty-four-hour things. I'm going to go home and get some sleep. See if I can shake it. I'm off tomorrow and Thursday. Hopefully, I'll be feeling better on Friday, okay? Thanks."

Cherry has an overnight bag. Hal finishes his beer and sets it on the counter.

He gives her an encouraging smile. "Ready?"

She nods.

"My car's in the alley."

She follows him out.

Hal opens the car door for her. Just as Cherry starts to get in, she stops.

"Damn," she says.

"What?"

"I forgot something. I'll be right back.

"Can I help?"

"No. Start the car. This'll take two minutes."

Cherry reenters the kitchen, puts her overnight bag on the counter, and unzips it. She removes the surgical gloves, slips them on, and pulls out a manila envelope and the duct tape. She reaches over and picks up Hal's beer bottle out of the trash. She carries the envelope, duct tape, and beer bottle into the living room. She places the bottle on the fireplace mantle. Then she removes the ransom note from the envelope, tears off a piece of duct tape, and tapes the note to the mantle. Then she picks up the fireplace poker, walks over to the gun case, and shatters the glass. She selects a handgun, opens a drawer, removes a handful of bullets, and puts the gun and the bullets into the manila envelope. She pauses to survey the room and then heads back to the kitchen, opens the cabinet beneath the sink, pulls the empty beer bottle out from behind the dishwasher detergent boxes, and sets it on the kitchen counter. Then she removes her surgical gloves, unzips her overnight bag, shoves them inside, zips the bag shut, and heads to the alley. She tosses her overnight bag in the backseat of Hal's car and gets in on the passenger side.

"All set?" he asks.

She nods. "All set."

"You say this motel is out by the airport?" he asks.

"It's a real dive. I've seen it on the way to the airport. Leonard will never think to look there."

Hal grins and shrugs. "Then off we go."

Hal guns the engine, shifts into Drive, and screeches out of the alley. His radio is on, the volume high.

He doesn't notice the late-model black Mustang parked down the street from Pitt's house, and certainly doesn't hear that engine start up.

Hal turns right at the corner and heads toward the highway. A moment later, the Mustang turns right at the corner and heads toward the highway.

• • ● • •

Thirty minutes later, we are inside the dingy front office of the Sleepy Time Motel. A jet screams by overhead in its final descent into Lambert Airport, momentarily drowning out the tinny sounds of *Gilligan's Island* coming from the portable TV visible in the back room behind the counter.

"Sixty, eighty—"

The elderly female day manager watches as Hal counts out twenty-dollar bills. She is dressed in a faded flowered housecoat. A lit cigarette dangles from the corner of her mouth. Easily in her seventies, she has jet black hair and a lacquered hairdo that could survive a direct hit from a cruise missile.

"—one-hundred, one-twenty, one-forty, one-sixty. There." Hal looks up and smiles. "Four nights, right?"

The day manager peers around Hal toward the parking lot. "Where's your wife."

"She's a little shy. Never stayed in a motel before. She's still in the car"

"Don't expect no one to clean your room. The maid quit. You want fresh towels or sheets, you bring the dirty ones down here and trade 'em for clean ones. Got that?"

"Sure do. Sounds good to me."

Twenty minutes later, Hal is sitting on the bed in Room 205. The bathroom door is closed.

"What?" Cherry calls from the bathroom.

"I said it seems a little depressing in here."

The bathroom door opens and Cherry emerges. She has on a man's dress shirt and black pumps. She walks over to the easy chair and leans against it, her backside toward Hal. Slowly moving her hips back and forth, she gradually lifts the tail of the shirt. She has nothing on underneath.

Looking back at Hal, she whispers, "Fuck me."

Chapter Thirteen

We are high above Tenth Street, inside the chambers of the Honorable Roy L. Stubbs, United States District Judge for the Eastern District of Missouri.

The room is imposing. Fit for a pharaoh, adequate for a federal judge. Tall ceilings, dark paneling, a huge picture window with a panoramic view of downtown St. Louis—of Busch Stadium, of the Old Courthouse framed by the Gateway Arch, of the Mississippi River. In front of that window sits a massive walnut desk. Behind that desk is a high-backed leather chair that's more throne than seat. And on that throne sits the Honorable Roy L. Stubbs, beads of sweat forming on his forehead.

His Honor leans to his right and releases another fart.

Fiber shock. Has to be. Christ Almighty, I'm going into fiber shock.

In the middle of the room, dominating the foreground, is a burled walnut conference table encircled by eight leather chairs. On one wall are floor-to-ceiling bookcases filled with bound law books. On another are portraits of Abraham Lincoln, Ronald Reagan, and George W. Bush, along with a framed St. Louis

University Law School diploma and a plaque displaying a bronzed Missouri State Highway Patrol badge. On the desk, a standup family portrait of a plump blond woman and three blond daughters, all wearing glasses. Hanging from a brass coatrack in the corner: a black robe and a bright orange-and-black plaid sports jacket.

His Honor lifts his haunches and releases another fart.

Married to a fiber zealot, for God's sake.

Yesterday morning Bernice had placed a homemade bran muffin next to his coffee mug. Had the heft of a waterlogged softball, the flavor of drywall. The Muffin from the Black Lagoon.

His Honor's stomach rumbles. Gas pressure builds again in his colon.

This morning she'd kissed him on the forehead and placed a bowl before him. He'd stared down at what looked like a pile of hamster turds.

"What in God's name are these?" he'd finally asked.

"Bran buds, Father. Packed with yummy fiber."

They'd tasted even worse than they looked, a moist blend of sawdust and industrial sand. His Honor had forced down half a bowl, all the while imagining what would happen if the president of Kellogg's ever found himself in the courtroom of U.S. District Judge Roy L. Stubbs.

His Honor shakes his head. Who'd have thought that the cute blonde he'd pulled over for speeding thirty-seven years ago on I-55 just south of Festus would become, in the thirty-third year of their marriage, a born-again believer in the divine grace of an ample bowel movement?

After three peaceful decades of Wonder Bread, Uncle Ben's, and Rice Krispies. Go figure.

Another wince, another fart.

Then again, he concedes, he isn't exactly the trim highway trooper anymore. When they were newlyweds she called him her John Wayne, although even then it was a reach for a guy five-foot-nine. It is far more of a reach now. Over the past thirty years he's added ten inches to his waistline, lost most of his hair, and padded those square jaws with a set of jowls. Last weekend at Home Depot, while selecting a new belt for the sander, he thought he'd spotted former Cubs manager Don Zimmer across the aisle—only to realize with a start that he was looking at his own reflection.

His Honor pulls a handkerchief from his back pocket and wipes the sweat off his forehead.

Definitely fiber shock.

There is a rap at the door.

"Christ," he mumbles, squeezing his butt cheeks together.

"It's open."

Into chambers lumbers His Honor's enormous docket clerk, Rahsan Abdullah Ahmed (né Lamar Williams). Six-feet-six-inches tall, two hundred eighty pounds, big as an ox, black as coal, and—on first impression—dumb as dirt. First impressions can be misleading.

"Good morning, Rahsan."

"Mornin', Yo' Honor."

Their first months together had been tough ones for Judge Stubbs. He enjoyed the pomp and circumstance of the district court, right down to the traditional *Oyez, Oyez, Oyez* to open court each morning. Thus he used to cringe when Rahsan banged the gavel three times and announced to the crowded courtroom, with a hearty *Oh-yeah, Oh-yeah, Oh-yeah, de United States Distick Coat is now in session!*

But that was then. Although Rahsan would never dub voice-overs for Darth Vader, it hadn't taken Judge Stubbs long to recognize his docket clerk's true value. He'd had *law* clerks, of course—those kids with degrees from snooty law schools. Even though they had all the street-smarts of a St. Louis Country Club dowager, those damn kids could research like there was no tomorrow, and that's important to former Highway Trooper Roy L. Stubbs. He isn't looking to blaze new paths in the law, especially after what the Eighth Circuit did to him last year in the *Arnold Bros.* appeal. Judge Eastman wrote the opinion for the panel. Made him sound like some yahoo who'd slipped his electronic cuffs, the pompous bastard. So these days he turns to his law clerks for the law. But when His Honor needs something more important than legal research, he has Rahsan. His law clerks occasionally let him down; they can't always find a precedent. But his docket clerk, God bless him, never lets him down.

"What do we have this morning?" Judge Stubbs asks.

Rahsan shakes his head with weary patience and tugs on his goatee. "Oh, jes' the usual tattletales and crybabies."

He hands Judge Stubbs the stack of motions that have been set for hearing that morning. His Honor checks his wristwatch and sighs. He could close his eyes and picture them: grim squadrons of lawyers armed with briefcases marching toward the Eagleton Courthouse, leaning forward with determination. Soon they'd be converging on the elevators below for their ascent to the courtrooms of Judge Stubbs and his fellow judges of the Eastern District of Missouri.

Morning motion call.

Judge Stubbs leafs through the all-too-familiar pile of papers, the distaste evident on his face. Motion to Compel Production of Documents. Motion for Extension of Time to File Reply Memorandum. Motion for Sanctions. Motion for Continuance. Motion to Compel Answers to Interrogatories. Motion for Sanctions. Motion for Leave to File Sur-Reply. Motion for Extension of Time to File Amended Complaint. Motion for Leave to File Brief in Excess of Twenty Pages. Motion for Continuance. Motion for Sanctions.

Same old crap.

Like most of his colleagues, Judge Stubbs detests the morning motion call. Sitting up there on the bench, listening to the parade of lawyers accusing each other of picayune violations of the rules, he feels like that old woman who lived in a shoe.

He looks up with a weary sigh. "Anything else?"

"Got ourselves an emergency motion, Judge. They seeking a T.R.O."

"Really? One of ours?"

"No, suh. Belong to Judge Weinstock."

"One of Marvin's cases? Why are they here?"

"He on vacation. This week and next."

"New case?"

"Not brand new, suh. Complaint filed last week."

"Last week? Why the rush?"

Rahsan shakes his head. "Don't know, Yo' Honor. Parties want a hearing. 'Specially the defendant. It's their motion for an expedited hearing on the plaintiff's motion. Presiding judge sent 'em down here."

"Am I the emergency judge this week?"

"Yes, suh. This week and next."

"The defendant's the one asking for a quick hearing, eh? That's a first." Judge Stubbs opens his desk calendar and studies it. "Well, looks like we can probably squeeze them in today. I have a pretrial conference at ten. Not much after that."

"I already tole 'em be here by eleven sharp."

Judge Stubbs looks up and smiles. "You have their motion papers?"

"Yes, suh. Right here." Rahsan Ahmed hands Judge Stubbs the court papers and stands up. "Motion call be startin' in ten minutes, Judge. I'll give a rap on the door when it's time."

Rahsan Ahmed lumbers out of Judge Stubbs' chambers just as Norman Feigelberg, one of the judge's law clerks, scurries into the reception area. Judge Stubbs' secretary has gone down the hall for another Diet Coke, and that leaves the two of them alone in the room. As usual, it's a bad hair day for Norman Feigelberg. With his kinky black hair (this morning mashed up to the right side) and his horn-rimmed glasses (the bridge repaired with white adhesive tape), Feigelberg could pass for the younger, myopic brother of Kramer on *Seinfeld*.

Feigelberg stares up at the docket clerk, squinting at him through thick lenses. "You just see the judge?"

"Yep."

Feigelberg nervously twists the bottom of his necktie around his index finger. "How's he feeling today?"

"It's that damn fiber." Rahsan wrinkles his nose. "Smell like something died in there. Po' mothafuckah fartin' to beat the band."

Feigelberg giggles, his head bobbing.

Rahsan steps back and waves his hand in front of his nose.

"On the subject of odors, Norman, you ain't exactly no rose yo'self."

"What's wrong?"

"Yo' breath is death."

Feigelberg grimaces. "I've got that darn gum infection again. I think it's a wisdom tooth."

"Here's some wisdom for you, baby. Get yo' ass down to Walgreens and bring back a gallon of Listerine, 'cause I don't intend to be smelling that stench all day."

Chapter Fourteen

Back inside chambers, Judge Stubbs grins as he rereads the complaint in *Mid-Continent Casualty Assurance Co. v. Leonard M. Pitt.*

He leans back and shakes his head.

Leonard Pitt.

It was twenty-one years ago, but he'll never forget that day. Started out as a lovely autumn morning—a lot like today. His first trial in the Circuit Court of the City of St. Louis. Oh, sure, he'd tried a few cases out in St. Charles County by then, and one down in Hillsboro, but this was the big-time. Better yet, he was going up against the famous Leonard Pitt.

More like the infamous. Even then, back all those years, back before mayoral candidate Leroy Robinson accused Pitt of being a member of "the cabal of evil men," Leonard Pitt had a reputation.

Leonard Pitt, eh?

Judge Stubbs grinned and nodded.

Might finally get a chance to nail the S.O.B.

On that morning twenty-one years ago, Roy Stubbs drove in from Festus, nervous but confident. Nervous because he was always nervous before a trial, and especially before this one. Even though he was several years older than Leonard Pitt, he was far less experienced. After all, Pitt was already trolling the halls of traffic court when Trooper Stubbs was attending his first night school class at St. Louis U Law School. But Stubbs was confident, too, because he had reason to be. He had the facts on his side. He had the law on his side. Better yet, he had evidence that Pitt's client had staged the accident. The whole thing was a fake, and he had a witness who could testify that Leonard Pitt had helped the plaintiff stage it.

Roy Stubbs fantasized on his drive downtown that morning: he would not only beat the great Leonard Pitt, he might even get the man hauled up on charges before the disciplinary commission. Yes, sir, he told himself on that lovely spring morning, the name Roy L. Stubbs would be in all the newspapers.

And it was. As the losing attorney in a one-hundred-forty-five-thousand-dollar judgment—at the time, the largest nonjury damage award in the history of the state of Missouri, and thus worth a front-page story in the *Post-Dispatch,* complete with a photograph of a beaming Leonard Pitt.

The trial had been an outrage from beginning to end. After the first hour—after Judge Madigan overruled every one of Stubbs' objections and granted Pitt's motion to exclude most of Stubbs' evidence—it finally dawned on Roy Stubbs: the fix was in. Worse yet, Madigan was a shrewd Irish fox who knew exactly how to throw a case while protecting his record on appeal.

The judge announced the verdict at the end of the second day of trial, immediately after Roy Stubbs finished his increasingly frantic closing argument. He'd sat numb at counsel's table while Pitt postured for the press outside the courtroom. He'd remained at counsel's table while Pitt and the judge met in chambers. He'd finally started packing up his court papers when Pitt emerged from the judge's chambers, puffing on a thick cigar.

Pitt had paused near Stubbs. "Tough luck, pal."

Stubbs had glared at him. "That wasn't luck. I know what you did."

Pitt smiled, the cigar clenched between his teeth. "This ain't the boonies, kid." He took the cigar out of his mouth, studied it for a moment, and took another puff. "Welcome to the big leagues."

Pitt had strolled out of the courtroom chuckling, trailing a wispy line of cigar smoke.

Welcome to the big leagues, eh, Leonard?

Judge Stubbs smiles.

Welcome to the big leagues, asshole.

Chapter Fifteen

Cherry holds the handgun with both hands, her arms outstretched, legs apart, slightly crouched. She is aiming at the bed in the motel room.

"Sorry, Hal."

She pulls the trigger.

Click.

And again.

Click.

The unmade bed is empty. Cherry is alone in the room.

She checked the Swiss account an hour ago. No money had been wired in.

The day after tomorrow is the deadline. If something goes wrong, if Leonard doesn't pay the ransom, Hal has to die. No other way. She needs to "escape" from her kidnapper, whose lips need to be sealed forever.

Cherry tosses the handgun onto the bed and checks her watch. Hal left to pick up coffee and rolls ten minutes ago. She needs to hurry. She takes the roll of duct tape out of her overnight bag, sits down in the armchair, and performs her daily routine. First, she tapes her bare ankles to the front legs of the chair, waits a few minutes, occasionally straining against the tape, and then leans down and unwraps the tape from each ankle. Then she tapes her left wrist to the left arm of the chair, waits a few minutes, occasionally straining against the tape, and then unwraps it. She then repeats that procedure with her right wrist. When she's finished, she shoves the crumpled pile of used duct tape under the bed.

She stands, stretches, and walks into the bathroom. She fills an empty cup with water and drinks it as she studies her face in the mirror. She still has the black eye. Using a piece of tissue paper, she scoops out some cold cream and rubs off the makeup. The black eye is gone. She turns on the shower, takes off her clothes and closes the bathroom door.

Above the muffled noise of the shower comes the sound of a high-pitched whir. It seems to be coming from inside the wall near the bed. The whirring sound grows louder, and suddenly a thick drill bit pokes through the wall just to the right of the bed at eye level. Still whirling, the drill bit moves slowly back and forth through the hole several times, almost erotically, and then withdraws, leaving a neat round hole about the size of a dime.

Chapter Sixteen

A knock on the door. "Motion time, Yo' Honor."

A moment later, Rahsan Ahmed lumbers into the courtroom to take up his position below the bench where Judge Stubbs presides. Rahsan stands at attention, eyes on the tall door to the left of the bench, the door that leads directly from Judge Stubbs' chambers into the courtroom. The gavel looks like a toy hammer in his huge hands.

Rahsan's mere presence in the courtroom commands obedience. The bone structure of his face gives him a natural scowl. Add to that his fierce eyes, and he seems to glower up there in a way that thoroughly intimidates all the lawyers with tassels on their loafers. You can see it in their eyes as they approach the podium during motion call, glancing over at him as if they're about to get clotheslined by the middle linebacker from Hell.

Like you and me, those nervous lawyers wish they could read Rahsan's mind. Not going to happen, though. Not for them, not for us.

Meanwhile, inside his chambers Judge Roy L. Stubbs stands by the coatrack, slipping on his black robe. He snaps it closed as he moves toward the courtroom door. Pausing a moment, he can't help but grin.

Welcome to the big leagues, Leonard.

His Honor turns the doorknob. That's Rahsan's signal. Through the door His Honor can hear the gavel pound three times. He hears Rahsan order everyone to rise.

The Honorable Roy L. Stubbs opens the door and steps into the courtroom.

Oh-yeah, Oh-yeah, Oh-yeah.

Forty-five minutes into the hearing Judge Stubbs decides he likes this Milton Bernstein. Nothing flashy, a bit of a nerd for sure, but he's getting the job done, one piece of evidence at a time.

"Objection, Judge. He's leading the witness."

Judge Stubbs looks over at Stan Budgah at defendant's table.

What the hell was the question?

Doesn't matter.

"Rephrase the question, Mr. Bernstein."

"Certainly, Your Honor."

Bernstein turns toward the witness. "Did Mr. Pitt say anything else, sir?"

Stan Budgah gives a grunt of satisfaction and sits back down.

Judge Stubbs glances down at his notes and frowns.

Stan Budgah? Really?

He knows Budgah from back in his days in private practice. This is probably Budgah's first appearance in federal court in years. Stan is strictly a ham-n-egger who mainly handles collection matters in state court. Probably the fattest collections lawyer in St. Louis. At least three hundred pounds. Judge Stubbs can hear Budgah's raspy, open-mouthed breathing all the way across the courtroom. Certainly dresses the part: shiny green sports jacket with a pair of cellophane-wrapped cigars—White Owls—sticking out of the breast pocket, a fat purple tie splotched with soup stains, a white short-sleeved Dacron shirt stretched over a big gut, gray wrinkled slacks with the crotch starting halfway down his massive thighs, scuffed black shoes, and a good two inches of hairy calf showing above the tops of his blue socks

Seated next to Stan Budgah at counsel's table is Leonard Pitt—tanned, trim, and immaculate in his gray pinstriped three-piece suit, blue oxford-cloth shirt, and red-on-navy club tie. He seems almost bored by the proceedings. Pitt could be Central Casting's answer to a call for a high-powered corporate litigator. Indeed, if someone were to walk into the courtroom cold, they would assume that Pitt was the lawyer and Budgah was the defendant, probably in a dirty bookstore prosecution.

As Judge Stubbs stares at him, Pitt looks up. Their eyes meet. Pitt gazes calmly, his face devoid of expression, not a hint of concern. It's unnerving. Even though Judge Stubbs is up on the bench, cloaked in judicial black, and vested with the might and authority of Article III of the United States Constitution, he is the one who breaks the stare. Flustered, he glances down at his notes.

"Your Honor." It's Bernstein. "We offer into evidence Plaintiff's Exhibit Six, the closing statement given to Mr. Ortega by Leonard Pitt on the date it bears."

Judge Stubbs turns toward Stan Budgah, who is in the process of heaving his bulk out of the chair. "Any objection, Counsel?"

Budgah squints and nods his head. "I'll object, Judge. I'll certainly object."

"On what grounds, Mr. Budgah?"

He waves *his* hand dismissively. "Relevance, materiality, best evidence rule, hearsay."

"Overruled. Exhibit Six is admitted into evidence, Mr. Bernstein."

"Thank you, Your Honor. I have no further questions for this witness."

"Any cross-examination, counsel?" Judge Stubbs asks.

Budgah starts to rise again when Pitt touches him on the shoulder. Budgah leans toward Pitt, who speaks softly in his ear. Budgah shrugs, and turns back to Judge Stubbs.

"Nothing, Judge."

Chapter Seventeen

Hal and Cherry are on the motel bed, both naked, their lovemaking over. Cherry is on her back. Hal is on his side facing Cherry, a confused look on his face.

"One million dollars?" he repeats.

"Yes, Hal."

"You're telling me he has to wire transfer a million dollars into a Swiss bank account by Friday at eleven a.m.? That's the day after tomorrow."

"Correct."

"You never told me any of this, Cherry."

"I'm sorry, baby. I was so freaked out. I never thought he would attack me like that. I was afraid, Hal. I didn't want to spook you. The money's for us, baby. I did it for us."

"Why would he agree to pay?"

"Fear."

"Fear of what?"

"Of me. That's the deal. He pays and I don't talk. It's worth it to him. My husband has done some very bad things, Hal. Enough to get him disbarred."

"Jesus, Cherry. It's practically blackmail. It might even be against the law."

Cherry gently touches Hal's cheek, her eyes watering. "Oh, sweetie, don't worry. All I'm trying to do is get out of this marriage with just a fraction of what I would have been entitled to except for that damn prenuptial agreement. That's not blackmail, that's justice."

Hal leans back, staring up at the ceiling. "Wow. I don't know."

"Think of all that money, Hal. You could quit school. We could do whatever we want. No more worries."

"Yeah, but it seems kind of risky."

"Not if we're careful, baby. That's why you can't make the call from here. I don't want anyone to know I'm here. Once we confirm the money has been wired, we're free."

"Maybe I should check with my brother, just to be safe. He's a lawyer. He can tell us whether this is legal."

"Don't worry. And don't even think of telling your brother. This is our secret. No one else can know. We'll be fine. I promise."

Hal sighs. "Okay. How do I call that Swiss bank?

Cherry smiles. "I'll get you the directions."

She leans over and kisses him on the lips. "My hero."

Chapter Eighteen

Judge Stubbs studies the document. After a few moments, he leans back in his chair and shakes his head. "Something's screwy here."

The three of them are in chambers—Judge Stubbs, Rahsan Ahmed, and Norman Feigelberg. Judge Stubbs had asked them to join him after he adjourned the hearing for a ninety-minute lunch recess.

Feigelberg pulls at his earlobe nervously. He looks at the judge, then at Rahsan, and then back at the judge. "I don't get it."

Rahsan grunts. "Norman, the man's stealing from both sides."

He gestures toward one of the exhibits the judge had brought back into chambers—a cancelled check. "He settle with the insurance for nineteen large but tells his client he settled for fourteen. Client don't know no better, insurance company don't know no better, and Ol' Leonard pocket the difference."

Judge Stubbs nods and turns toward Norman.

"His clients are easy marks, Norman. Poor blacks and Hispanics. Those are the folks most likely to be intimidated by the legal system."

The judge turns back to Rahsan and shakes his head. "But still, it doesn't make sense."

"What doesn't?" Feigelberg asks.

Rahsan turns to Feigelberg. "Stan Budgah."

Feigelberg frowns. "Why?"

"In this kind of case, Norman," Judge Stubbs says, "Pitt ought to be represented by the best lawyer he can afford, and trust me, he can afford the very best."

"Man could hire Clarence Darrow. Should hire Clarence Darrow." Rahsan tugs pensively on his mustache. "It like he don't care."

"Maybe he and Budgah are close," Feigelberg suggests.

Rahsan snorts. "And maybe I'm the chocolate Easter Bunny."

His Honor's stomach rumbles audibly. He casts a furtive glance toward the lunch bag resting on the corner of the couch by the large picture window. Inside will be yet another tomato-and-sprouts sandwich on her homemade high-fiber special—two dense slices of bread bristling with those damn wheat flakes that look and taste like burlap.

Rahsan glances at his judge and stands.

"Come on, Norman," he says. "We got work to do."

Out in the hall, Feigelberg says, "But what about lunch?"

Rahsan shakes his head. "Forget about lunch, Norman. We don't have time for that shit. I'll go downstairs to the clerk's office and check the federal dockets. I can't leave the building 'cause I got to be here when court resumes. That means you going to have to get your ass over to the Circuit Court and sweet-talk one of them clerks to run his name through every docket in the fucking building. Every single one, Norman. Anybody got a suit against Leonard Pitt in the Circuit Court of the City of St. Louis, I want to know about it. You understand me?"

Feigelberg nods with resignation. "Yeah, yeah."

Rahsan checks his watch. "We be starting up again at one-thirty. I'm guessing they be *putting* on evidence 'til three. You make sure you back here before then, Norman."

"What's the rush?"

Rahsan's eyes widen. "What you smoking, son? This here is an emergency motion. They want our judge to freeze the man's assets. Every last penny."

"So?"

"I got a feeling our judge gonna wanna to do that." Rahsan pauses. "For some reason, our judge got himself a big ol' hard-on for Mr. Leonard M. Pitt, Esquire."

Rahsan shakes his head. "'Fore I let him enjoin the man, I gotta know if there's something out there in the weeds gonna jump up and bite us in the ass. So get a move on, Norman. Time's a wastin'"

● ● ● ● ●

Neither Rahsan nor Norman found anything of import. Pitt had been a plaintiff a few times, and a defendant twice, but the disputes had all been over alleged breaches of contract having absolutely no bearing on the case before them.

Judge Stubbs turns to Stan Budgah. "What about defendant?"

Budgah turns to Pitt, who shakes his head.

Budgah heaves himself out of his chair and faces the bench. "Defendant has nothing further, Judge."

"Very well," Judge Stubbs says, pausing to close his notebook and put down his pen. "Will the defendant rise?"

Down below, Rahsan Ahmed clears his throat.

Leonard Pitt stands, his expression almost serene.

"Mr. Pitt," Judge Stubbs begins in a God-of-the-Old-Testament voice, "this court is profoundly disturbed by the evidence presented this afternoon."

He pauses.

Pitt gazes at him, unruffled, his eyes distant, as if he is listening to a piano concerto instead of the preamble to a federal injunction.

Judge Stubbs frowns.

"Yes," His Honor finally says, aiming for a stern tone, "profoundly disturbed."

Rahsan Ahmed clears his throat louder this time.

Judge Stubbs pauses and glances down at his docket clerk. The two exchange a silent look.

"Ah, yes," Judge Stubbs says, turning toward the lawyers with a slightly perplexed expression. "The court, uh, will be in recess, gentlemen."

He checks his watch. "It's three-twenty. We will reconvene shortly."

• ● ● ● •

They are alone in chambers, just the judge and Rahsan. Norman Feigelberg stands at the door, waiting. He isn't trying to eavesdrop, but he can't help but hear.

The judge crosses his arms defiantly over his chest. "I'm gonna burn his ass."

Rahsan nods calmly. He walks slowly, pensively, toward the picture window.

Judge Stubbs turns in his chair, following his enormous docket clerk with his eyes. Rahsan tugs on his goatee as he meditates on the view of the Mississippi River. He knows his judge. He knows enough to let this silence linger a bit longer. When enough time has passed, he turns toward Judge Stubbs.

"I'm worried the man is using you," he says in a quiet voice.

"Using me?" Judge Stubbs gives him an incredulous stare. "Using me for what?"

The docket clerk shakes his head. "Don't know the answer yet."

"Come on, Rahsan. He's the defendant here. He's the one who got hauled into court."

Rahsan shrugs, keeping his posture non-confrontational, "The man's an opportunist, Yo' Honor. He didn't set up the lawsuit, but look what he done so far: got this hearin' switched to you, hired that tub of lard to represent him—all to make sure he gonna lose this motion."

Judge Stubbs scratches his neck. "I appreciate your concern, Rahsan. But this is bigger than all that. Don't you see? Leonard Pitt is defrauding that insurance company, and he's stealing from his clients. Good God, man, he's violating federal laws. What am I supposed to do? Look the other way? Let him continue to prey on the public?"

Rahsan shrugs. "Man been preying on the public for twenty-five years. Couple mo' weeks ain't gonna destroy the country."

"Oh, come on, Rahsan. We can't take that attitude. This is a court of law."

Rahsan walks slowly back across the room and stops in front of the desk. He places his massive fists on the desk and leans forward, towering over Judge Stubbs. Rahsan stares down at his judge, his dark eyes as focused as laser beams. "I'm just worried that man is using you."

Stubbs smiles. "Don't worry about me, Rahsan. I'm a big boy. I've been waiting a long time for this moment. And I'm going to enjoy it."

• • ● • •

With a flourish, Judge Stubbs signs three copies of the order he's just read aloud. He hands them down to his docket clerk and watches as Rahsan gives one to Stan Budgah and one to Milton Bernstein. Bernstein remains at the podium, rereading the last two paragraphs of the order. Budgah returns to the defendant's table, where Pitt snatches the two-page order from him.

"Gentlemen," Judge Stubbs says, "Judge Weinstock will be back from vacation in two weeks. The injunction will remain in effect until his return. If any procedural issues should arise before then, you can contact Judge Weinstock's docket clerk."

He pauses, his eyes on Milton Bernstein. "Any questions?"

Bernstein is grinning. "None, Your Honor."

Judge Stubbs turns toward defendant's table. "Mr. Budgah?"

Budgah looks at the judge, glances warily at his client, and then back at the judge. "Uh, I think we're okay."

"Very good." Judge Stubbs closes his notebook and stands up. "We'll be in recess."

Rahsan bangs the gavel. *"All* rise!"

Judge Stubbs pauses at the door, his hand on the knob, and turns back. Pitt is still seated at defendant's table, the order clenched in his hands.

Pitt looks up. Their eyes meet, and for that moment there is no one else in the room. All of those intervening years vanish, but this time it is Pitt seated at counsel's table. He glares at Judge Stubbs, who gazes back serenely. And this time it is Pitt who breaks the stare. He looks down at the order. Judge Stubbs waits a beat, wishing only that he had a cigar, and then he pushes through the door and disappears.

Oh-yeah, Oh-yeah, Oh-yeah.

• • ● • •

Two hours later, we are inside Lawrence Armstrong's office at Abbott & Windsor. It's crowded with celebrants—several from the firm, two executives from Mid-Continent Casualty Insurance Company. Lawrence is sipping on a glass of champagne, shaking hands, slapping backs, feeling good.

Milton Bernstein strides into the room, a triumphant grin on his face.

"Ah," Lawrence announces, "the man of the hour. Well, Milton? Fill us in."

Milton nods, still grinning. "We served the final bank with notice at four-forty-three this afternoon. As of the close of business today, all liquid assets of Leonard Pitt are frozen. Mission accomplished!"

Cheers and applause. High fives.

Milton clenches his fist over his head and starts chanting, "Attica! Attica! Attica!"

Chapter Nineteen

The following morning, Leonard Pitt is seated at his desk, the phone cradled between his shoulder and his ear. He calmly puffs on a Montecristo No. 2 cigar. Yes, the Cuban version.

Harvey Abrams is on the other end of the call. Harvey is a senior vice president at Merchant's Bank, and he is clearly agitated.

"I just don't know what to say, Mr. Pitt."

"But what about that wire transfer, Harvey? I'm going to need to transfer that money this afternoon. It's literally a matter of life and death, Harvey. No bullshit."

"I'm terribly sorry, Mr. Pitt. Our paperwork is all done, we are ready to go, but the bank's hands are tied by that darn court order. We can't do a thing about it. I feel so bad about this whole thing. I just don't know what to say.

"I'm disappointed in you, Harvey. You and your bank."

"But Mr. Pitt—"

Pitt hangs up. He turns toward the picture window behind his desk and surveys the Arch from twenty stories up. He takes another puff of his cigar and presses a button on the phone console. A moment later, Belinda

walks in. Pitt eyes her with appreciation. She looks par-
ticularly sexy this morning in her tight sweater, short
leather skirt, and spike heels.

"What's up, Len?"

Pitt takes the cigar out of his mouth, studies it for a
moment, and then swivels his chair toward the window.
"Get Captain O'Brien on the phone."

"Okay."

She doesn't move.

"Now," Pitt says, still gazing out the window. "Get
him now."

"Len?"

"What?"

"I was just wondering."

Pitt swivels his chair back toward her. "Wondering
what?"

"That darn lawsuit. I mean, what are you going to
do? The money's all tied up?"

"Don't worry. I've already fired Budgah. I'll have
a new lawyer by tomorrow. I'll have that order lifted
next week."

"But aren't you worried?"

Pitt nods. "I'm concerned. But I have more important matters on my mind now. That's why I asked you
to get Captain O'Brien on the phone. Now."

Belinda turns to leave but pauses at the door."

"Len?"

Pitt sighs. "What now?"

"You want me to come in after the call? It's Thursday, you know." She raises her eyebrows. "I wore your
favorite panties."

"Not today. For chrissake, Belinda, get O'Brien on the goddamn telephone. Now."

Belinda flounces out of the room. Pitt turns back to the window and puffs on his cigar.

A minute later, there's a buzz on his intercom line. Pitt presses the speaker button. "Yes?"

"Captain O'Brien," Belinda says, her voice twenty degrees colder than before. "Line three."

Pitt lifts the receiver. "Jim?"

"Hey there, Leonard, how's tricks?

"Not good, pal. You're not going to believe this."

"What's up?"

"Some bastard kidnapped my wife."

Chapter Twenty

Ten miles to the west, Hal is seated on the bed in his apartment. He's on his cell phone, a sheet of notes on his lap.

On the other end of the phone, a male voice with a Swiss accent says, "Okay. And now I will need the personal identification number, please."

"Sure. Let's see…that would be five-six-seven-five-nine-nine."

"One moment please." A pause. "Okay. Your inquiry, sir?"

"Yeah, uh, give me the account balance, okay? In U.S. dollars."

"One moment, please…Current balance in account one-one-three-five-two-eight-six in U.S. dollars is eleven-thousand-two-hundred-three dollars and sixty-seven cents."

"That's all?"

"Yes, sir. That is accurate."

"No deposits today?"

"No, sir. No account activity."

"Jesus."

"Pardon, sir?"

"Nothing. Thanks, dude."

"You are must welcome, sir."

Hal ends the call and drops the phone onto the bed. "Damn."

Chapter Twenty-one

The next morning—Friday—Hal and Patty are at the pool area entrance checking membership cards.

"Your brother looks nothing like you," she says.

"Huh?"

"Your brother. Milton, right? He looks nothing like you."

"My brother? Where'd you see my brother?"

"On TV, silly."

"When?"

"Last night."

"What are you talking about?"

"Didn't you watch the news?"

"Oh, my God. What happened to him?"

"Nothing bad, Hal. It's all good. He won some big lawsuit. They filmed him coming out of the courthouse. They asked him a question or something. I can't believe you didn't watch your brother on TV. Maybe you can find the clip on the Internet."

"What kind of lawsuit?"

"I can't remember. Something about some big-shot lawyer getting sued or something."

Hal stands. "I'll be right back."

He heads into the pool area and over to the lifeguard office. One of the other lifeguards—a college kid name Brian—is leaning back on a folding chair listening to music on his iPod.

Hal taps him on the shoulder. "You got today's paper?"

Brian nods toward the desk, where today's *St. Louis Post-Dispatch* sits, unopened as usual.

Hal picks it up, separates the front page section, and spots the story below the fold. His eyes widen.

"Oh, no!"

He runs out of the office with the newspaper in his hand.

• • ● • •

At that same time, Cherry emerges from the motel bathroom, fresh from her shower and wrapped in a white towel. Her face momentarily registers surprise, but she quickly recovers.

"How long has he known?" she asks.

"A while."

She nods. "He paying you extra for this?"

A shrug. "We ain't worked out the details."

"I'll double it. The job's worth fifty grand."

"Fifty? How you figure?"

"We get out of here. Go somewhere safe. You call him. Tell him you want a hundred to keep quiet. He'll pay. He has to. We split it fifty-fifty."

"A hundred, huh?"

"Yep."

"What about that dumbass lifeguard?

"Kill him."

"Which you was planning to do all along, weren't ya, Cherry?"

She just gazes at him. After a moment, she shrugs.

"Hundred, huh?" he says. "And all I get is fifty."

"You get a lot more than that."

She takes two steps toward him as she loosens the towel. She lets it drop to the carpet as she gets down on her knees in front of him. She stares up at him and then nods toward his crotch. "More than he ever got."

He unzips his fly. "Yeah?"

"Yeah. Oh, my. Look at that."

"Not bad, eh?"

"So big! So yummy!"

Chapter Twenty-two

The traffic on Highway 70 is bumper to bumper, red brake lights as far ahead as Hal can see. Some sort of accident up ahead. He shakes his head, exasperated. Tapping on the steering wheel, Hal glances down again at the passenger seat, where the *Post-Dispatch* is open to the front page.

ST. LOUIS LAWYER SUED FOR FRAUD JUDGE FREEZES ASSETS

A St. Louis federal judge entered an order yesterday afternoon tying up the assets of Leonard Pitt, a prominent St. Louis attorney accused of fraud in a multi-million dollar lawsuit filed by a Chicago insurance company.

• • ● • •

"I cannot believe this," Hal says aloud. "I. Cannot. Believe. This."

Thirty minutes later, he pulls his car into the motel lot below Cherry's second-floor room. He turns off the engine, gets out, and takes two deep breaths, trying to figure out exactly how the break the news. He walks up the stairs and down the deck to her room. He pauses, takes a breath, and knocks.

"It's me, babe," he calls. "I got some bad news."

No answer.

He knocks again. "Cherry? It's Hal. Open up."

No answer. He presses his ear against the door, tries the handle. He reaches into his pocket for the key.

"Damn."

He goes back downstairs to his car, opens the glove compartment, and takes out the extra room key. As he straightens up a jet passes overhead in its final descent. The ground shudders as the plane screams past. He turns to watch it land, momentarily tempted to bolt, just get the hell out of here, maybe back to California. He turns back to the motel, stares up at Cherry's door. With a sigh and a shake of his head, he starts back toward the stairway.

He knocks again at the door. "Cherry? It's Hal. Open up, babe."

The distant roar of another approaching plane can be heard. The sounds of the jet engines grow louder as Hal inserts the key. The metal guardrail begins vibrating from the noise. As the jet passes overhead, its engines screaming, Hal opens the door.

Stage 2:
The Pivot

Chapter Twenty-three

Saturday morning.

Milton wakes to the cooing of a pigeon on the ledge outside the bedroom window. The digital alarm clock on the nightstand reads 7:35 AM. Milton turns to Peggy. She is asleep on her stomach, her head turned away, her left arm resting in the space between their pillows. The bed sheet is below her waist. She is wearing a white cotton nightshirt.

Milton runs his lips tenderly along her forearm. Peggy sighs and shifts slightly. Milton turns on his side facing her and moves his fingers along the back of her neck and through her hair. Peggy turns to face him with a sleepy smile.

She reaches over and touches his check. "Think we have enough time?"

Milton squints. "I don't hear them."

She reaches under the sheet and moves her hand down his waist.

"My goodness. Someone's ready."

She moves on top of Milton and nips him gently on the nose. "Let's go, stud."

She reaches back and pulls the sheet over them.

She winks. "Just in case."

She kisses him. "Mmm, you smell delicious, Milton."

Peggy stiffens.

"What?" Milton says.

"Shit," she whispers, and rolls off him.

The bedroom door bursts open and in charge their two daughters. Both are still in their pajamas, but each has donned a princess tiara. The older one—Sara, age seven—is holding a toy scepter.

"Good morning, Your Highnesses," Sara announces in a cheerful voice.

"Morning girls," Milton says.

The younger one—Maddy, age five—says, "Hi, Daddy. Hi, Mommy."

Peggy sits up in bed and smiles. "Good morning, Princess Maddy."

"Daddy," Sara says, "can we have breakfast?"

"You certainly can."

"Is it a weekend, Daddy?" Maddy asks.

"You are correct, Maddy. It is Saturday morning."

Maddy turns to Sara, eyes lit up. "Cartoons!"

Sara screams. "Cartoons!"

Both girls start jumping up and down.

"Listen, girls," Milton says. "Go on downstairs. Daddy will be right down. You can eat breakfast in the den and watch cartoons, okay?"

"Awesome!" Sara shouts. "Come on, Maddy!"

They charge out of the bedroom.

Milton turns to Peggy. "I'll fix them up with cold cereal. The cartoons ought to hold them for an hour. Don't go away. I'll be back in five."

"Hurry up, or I'll start without you."

Downstairs in the den the girls are watching cartoons. Milton walks in holding a box of Wheaties and a box of Kix

"Which one, girls. Wheaties or Kix?"

"Oatmeal!" Maddie shouts.

"Oatmeal!" Sara shouts.

"Oatmeal?" Milton repeats. He turns and starts toward the kitchen. Under his breath he grumbles, "Shit."

Five minutes later, Milton is getting the breakfast trays ready. There is a container of oatmeal on the counter along with a bottle of milk, a jar of honey, and a carton of orange juice. The microwave Dings! Milton yanks open the microwave door and starts to reach in.

"Oh, shit."

Both bowls of oatmeal have bubbled over the top. The microwave is a mess.

He glances over at the kitchen clock. "Shit, shit, shit."

He steps out to the stairway. "Five more minutes, Peggy."

Five more minutes, and now Milton is peering through the glass door of the microwave, intently watching the rotating bowls. The phone rings.

"I got it," Sara shouts from the den.

The microwave Dings!

Milton yanks open the door and smiles. "Ah, yes."

A minute later, Milton comes into the den with the two trays. Each has a bowl of oatmeal and a glass of orange juice. Sara is still on the phone as Milton sets the trays down.

She turns to her father. "It's Uncle Hal, Daddy."

Milton takes the phone. "You're sure up early."

"Oh, man. I've been up for a while. The cops woke me at four in the morning."

"Who woke you?"

"The cops."

"Where are you?"

"The police station. In one of their interrogation rooms."

"The police station? Why?"

"I'm under arrest."

"What's the charge?"

"You ready for this? Kidnapping and murder.

"What? Is this your idea of a joke?"

"I wish. Jeez, Bro, they arrested me at four in the morning. They searched my apartment."

"Did they have a warrant?"

"I think so. Maybe. I don't know. It was four in the morning, man."

Milton turns toward the television, where one of those bizarrely violent cartoons is in progress: the coyote has just dashed off the cliff and come to a halt in midair, looks down, eyebrows raised, and then plummets a hundred yards, landing in a pool of water.

"Kidnapping?"

Hal sighs. "Yep. And murder."

"Who?"

"This gal. Her name's Cherry Pitt."

Milton sits down on the edge of the couch.

"Milton? You still there?"

"She's dead?"

"I'm in deep shit, man. Deep."

"What are the cops doing?"

"They got a detective named Moran. He's been trying to get a statement out of me."

"Have you told him anything?"

"Not much."

"Tell him you're waiting for your lawyer. Don't tell him anything else. Nothing, Hal. Not a thing. Wait for me. I'm coming right down."

Chapter Twenty-four

We are now in the lobby of the police headquarters. Ten minutes to noon. Milton is up at the front desk, jabbing his finger at the fat bald desk sergeant.

"I have now been here exactly one hour, Sergeant. I assume you have been fully briefed on the Supreme Court's 1966 holding in Miranda v. Arizona, which can be found at 384 U.S. 486. Pardon my French, Sergeant, but quit jerking me around."

"Sorry, sir. Had a shift change. Still trying to confirm he's up there."

"Exactly where else would he be? Riding the Screaming Eagle at Six Flags?"

"Like I say, sir, just trying to confirm he's up there."

Milton walks back over to the hard bench and sits down, shaking his head. "Unbelievable."

"Don't feel bad."

Milton looks over at a skinny guy in his early forties with longish black hair and bags under his eyes. He's wearing khakis and a short-sleeved white shirt. There's a small notepad sticking out of his shirt pocket.

"Bad about what?" Milton asks.

"O'Bannon. He does it to every lawyer."

"Who are you?"

"Peters. *Post-Dispatch*. You Bernstein's attorney?

Milton nods.

"Not a criminal lawyer, are you?"

"Not usually."

"I could tell. O'Bannon'll play dumb for a couple hours. Give the dicks a chance to get your client to talk. When they give up, O'Bannon will suddenly locate your client."

"How do you know my client's up there?"

Peters chuckled. "I've been covering St. Louis County courts for six years, pal. This is the kind of case we call a heater. A kidnapping and a murder. Better yet, the victim is Leonard Pitt's wife. It'll be a media circus down here in a couple hours, Counselor. You're going to get one hell of an introduction to criminal law."

Milton's eyes widen. "Did you say Leonard Pitt's wife?"

Peters nods. "Yep. Like I say, a heater."

Milton leans back against the wall and shakes his head. "Excellent."

"Here comes Moran. He's the dick on the case."

Detective Bernie Moran walks into the waiting area. He's dark and stocky, with black hair and a Fu Manchu mustache. He's wearing khaki slacks and a Chicago White Sox T-shirt. He nods at Peters and looks at Milton.

"You Harold S. Bernstein's lawyer?"

"That is correct, sir. And who are you?"

Moran shrugs. "Come with me, Counselor. Your client would like to see you."

They ride the elevator in silence and get off at the third floor. Milton follows Moran down the hall to a steel door labeled Interview Room C.

Moran turns to Milton and shakes his head. "Got yourself a real pervert for a client.

"Oh? And what is your definition of a pervert?"

Moran pauses, hand on the doorknob. "How 'bout a guy who'd put a bullet in a naked woman's head, shoot his wad in her mouth, and put out his cigarette on one of her tits? I'd say that's just a little beyond Mister Rogers' Neighborhood."

He opens the door and smiles. "He's all yours, Counselor."

Chapter Twenty-five

Milton stares at the airshaft through the barred window. He turns to Hal, who is sitting at the table, handcuffed, the cuffs bolted to the table.

"She was on the bed?"

"Yeah. There was blood everywhere. Her eyes were open. Jesus, Milton. It was horrible. I almost threw up, Bro."

"You didn't see anyone?"

"No one. I ran back to the car and got out of there as fast as I could. I threw the room key out the window on the highway."

"What did she do during the day out there?"

"I don't know. She said she watched TV or read magazines. I was with her most of the day on Wednesday and Thursday. My days off."

"On the day you drove her out to the motel—you saw her house, right?

"Yeah. The living room was a mess. She had a black eye. Her old man beat her up."

"Was there a note taped to the fireplace mantle?"

Hal frowns, trying to remember. "I don't think so."

Milton comes over to the table and sits next to his little brother.

"They're going to take you over to bond court. I'll be there for you. If they have enough to charge you, the bond's going to be high. I'll do what I can."

Hal shakes his head, tears in his eyes. "What a mess, Milton. A total clusterfuck. What am I going to do?"

"You're going to hold yourself together in here. I'm going to find out what happened."

"I didn't do anything, Milton. There was no kidnapping. She had me drive her out there. I'm innocent. I swear."

"I know."

"I'm scared, Bro."

Milton squeezes his younger brother's shoulder. "Someone killed her, Hal. Killed her and set you up. I won't let it happen. I promise."

Chapter Twenty-six

In the detective squad room, Detective Bernie Moran is sipping coffee from a thick, stained mug, his feet up on the edge of his metal desk. He stares at Milton, who stands across the desk from him.

"What do you have on him?" Milton asks.

"It'll be in my report. Should be ready on Monday, Counselor. You can get it from the prosecutor."

"I'd prefer to know now."

"And I'd prefer season tickets to the Cardinals games. Preferably first row behind the dugout." Moran shakes his head. "Fucking lawyers. You know the drill. What makes you think you deserve special treatment?"

Milton stares at him. "Because he's my brother."

Moran squints. "Your brother, eh?" He leans back in his chair and frowns. "Harold S. Bernstein. Wait… wait a minute. Hal Bernstein."

"Yes, Hal Bernstein. My brother."

"Jesus Christ." He lowers his legs and sits up straight. "Hal Bernstein? That Hal Bernstein?'

"What Hal Bernstein?"

"Used to play ball?"

Milton sighs. "Yes. Yes, you are correct. Why is that of interest here?"

"Pitcher. Mizzou, right?"

"Yes, Detective Moran, my brother attended the University of Missouri on a baseball scholarship."

Moran grins and tugs at his Fu Manchu. "That's the guy, eh? Holy shit. I remember him back then. I was down at Champaign. Catcher. We played Mizzou. In that tournament in Iowa my senior year. Your brother was a sophomore then, I think."

Milton rolls his eyes. "Maybe."

"Son of a bitch pitched one helluva game. Dude had fucking control like I've never seen. Never before, never since. Our coach called it Barnum and Bailey control. Your brother, eh? He was a goddamn legend in college baseball back then. I shit you not. What did he have that day against us? Fifteen strikeouts?"

"I have no idea. I was attending law school in Chicago at the time."

"Best goddamn pitcher I ever faced. Ever. Figured he'd be in majors by now. What happened?"

"Motorcycle accident. Severely damaged his shoulder."

"That's tough, man. He ever play since?"

"You'd have to ask him."

Moran grinned and shook his head. "Yeah, right. He'll tell me I have to ask his lawyer. So now I'm asking his fucking lawyer. He ever play since?"

Milton forced a smile. "He told me he might have a chance to start pitching some. I think it might involving throwing batting practice to some minor league team across the river."

"The Grizzlies?"

"That may be their name. And you, Detective? What about you and our so-called National Pastime?"

"Me?" Moran chuckles. "I was never in your brother's league. Just softball these days. Police league. Bunch of knuckleheads. Not the same. Different sport."

Milton took a seat facing Moran. "Tell me about my brother."

Moran mulls it over. "It'll all be in my report anyway. No harm telling you a couple days early. Your little brother's in bad shape. We can place him at the scene of the kidnapping. That took place at the house. We were able to lift his prints off a beer bottle near the ransom note. An easy match. He certainly hasn't lost his cool from his baseball days. Drinks a beer after he kidnaps that woman. The ransom note was duct taped over the fireplace. The check-out girl at the Walgreens near your brother's apartment says she thinks she sold him a roll of it around the time of the kidnapping. We confirmed that from the credit card receipt in the motel room. His credit card."

Moran shakes his head. "Not the brightest move there. Anyway, we found a half-used roll of duct tape in the motel room and a pile of used tape shoved under the motel bed. The medical examiner found traces of it on the skin of her ankles and wrists, all of which show abrasions from what appears to be her straining against that tape. Looks like she was taped to the armchair in the room. And, yeah, I'm pretty sure we'll be able to place him at the murder scene. The lab guys were able to lift several prints at the motel room and what looks like semen from the bedsheets. We'll have their report early next week. Ballistics says the bullet came from the handgun the kidnapper stole from Pitt's house. The lab is checking the semen samples from the bedsheets and from inside her mouth. We'll know if it matches your brother's blood type Monday."

"Her mouth?"

"Yeah. I'm guessing she either gave him a blow job or he jerked off after her shot her. And then he tried to wipe it off. He got almost all of it, but there are still traces."

Milton absorbs the information in silence. Finally, he asks, "Anything else?"

Moran chuckles. "Oh, yeah. A homicide dick's dream. We found two *Time* magazines and four *Sports Illustrated*s under the couch in your brother's room. The *Sports Illustrated*s had his subscription label on them."

The phone on Moran's desk rings. He answers it. "Moran...yeah...okay."

He starts taking notes. "Okay... right...got it."

He hangs up and looks at Milton. "They just pulled your brother's cell phone account. Mrs. Pitt was kidnapped on Tuesday. The ransom money was supposed to be wire transferred to a Swiss bank on Friday. According to the phone company records, someone made a long distance call to that bank on Thursday afternoon from your brother's cell phone."

Moran opens a manila folder on his desk and sorts through several eight-by-ten photographs. He hands one to Milton. "The victim."

Milton takes the photo as Moran's phone starts to ring.

Milton stares at the photo. It's a shot of Cherry Pitt, naked, on her back on the bed, arms at her sides, legs bent at the knees and hanging over the bed. There is a hole in her forehead, slightly off center to the left. The sheets around her head are stained dark. Her eyes are open.

Moran hangs up and turns to Milton. "You want to see the other shots?"

"Not now. What about those magazines you mentioned? How are they relevant?"

"Oh, yeah. We found them under your brother's couch. Each had a couple pages missing—torn out. We got complete copies of each magazine from the library. We compared the missing pages to the ransom note."

"And?"

"And the kidnapper made the ransom note by cutting and pasting words and letters from magazines. The words and letters from the ransom note match up exactly—EXACTLY—with the words and letters from the missing pages of those magazines."

Moran pauses and shakes his head. "Sorry to break the news, Mr. Bernstein, but your brother is fucked. Totally. You better hope the prosecutor is in the mood to cut a deal. Otherwise, he's going away for life—assuming you can help him avoid the death penalty."

Chapter Twenty-seven

Here we are, in the Law Office of Herschel P. Goldman, P.C.

Yes, *that* Herschel Goldman. The one and only. Maybe you've seen that billboard on Highway 70—the one featuring the photo of the sixty-something attorney with the gray handlebar mustache, the fat red bowtie, and the comb-over. Or more likely, one of those cheesy late-night TV commercials, each featuring the same trademark sign-off: "Come see the Goldman." Pronounced "Gold...Man." The most recent one has him standing in front of that wrecked, overturned car, the windows shattered, steam rising from the engine. "If you've been injured," he says, "someone somewhere out there owes you a pile of gold. That's why I'm here. Come see the Gold Man." It closes, as they all do, with Herschel Goldman twirling one end of his gray mustache as he winks into the camera.

Herschel Goldman also happens to be Uncle Heschie to Milton's wife, Peggy. He's Peggy's mother's older brother. His law practice consists of a hodgepodge of criminal and civil cases—everything from felonies to fender-benders, from DUIs to divorces—all conducted

out of a second-floor office above Mound City Pawn
Shop on North Jefferson Avenue.

But don't get fooled by the surroundings or the clients
or those cheesy television commercials. The namesake of
the Law Office of Herschel P. Goldman, P.C. graduated
at the top of his law school class at St. Louis University,
back when none of the big firms in town hired Jews.
That was fine by him. As his proud father, Moishe, *alav
ha shalom*, used to tell his buddies (aka the *alter kockers*)
at the Kiddush after Shabbat services at Bais Abraham
Synagogue, "That boy of mine, Herschel, he's not only
got *seykhel* but a real *Yidisher kop*." Or, as the managing
partner of the largest insurance defense firm in town said
two days ago, when his paralegal brought him a copy
of a new lawsuit filed against one of his clients and he
flipped to the signature block on the last page of the
pleading, "Oh, shit. Not him again."

On this weekday morning, the Gold Man looks up
from the papers on his desk and smiles.

"Ah, Miltie," he says with just a hint of a sing-song
Yiddish accent, gesturing with the other hand toward
the chair in front of his desk. "Sit, *boychik*."

Milton sits.

"*Nu?*" Herschel twirls one end of his handlebar mustache. "What can I do for my nephew-in-law?"

"I need a good investigator."

Herschel nods. "Okay. Define good."

"Reputable, dependable, solid credentials, access to
a lab."

"You need reputable, eh?"

"Definitely. I may need him to testify."

Herschel twists his mustache as he mulls it over. "Reputable."

He turns toward the credenza and begins flipping through his huge, circular Rolodex. "Reputable...reputable...ah, here we are."

He removes a card from the Rolodex and turns back toward Milton.

"I have your man, Miltie." He hands the card to Milton. "Fred Butz. B-U-T-Z.I don't always need reputable, but when I do, Butz is my man."

Milton studies the card. "Who is he?"

"President and sole employee of Butz Investigations."

Milton raises his eyebrows. "Sounds like a proctologist."

"An old joke, Miltie. Poor Fred's heard it at least a million times, maybe more. However infelicitous his name may be, Fred Butz has impressive credentials. A genuine maven, I kid you not. A former FBI special agent with a master's degree in chemistry. Does his own lab work. Very reliable. What kind of case?"

"Criminal."

"White collar?"

"No. Murder and kidnapping."

"Oy." Herschel winces. "Your poor brother? You're representing him?"

"For now."

"Leonard Pitt's wife, eh?"

"I know. I'm suing him. We got a judge to freeze his assets."

"That was you, eh? Good for you. Couldn't happen to a more deserving fellow than Pitt. That man is a real *mamzer.*"

"There's a hearing on the case later this morning. He's retained new lawyers, too."

"Who was his lawyer before?"

"Sam Budgah."

Herschel raises his eyebrows. "Sam? Really?"

"Not anymore. He has a team of litigators from Warren and London, a big Chicago firm. They filed more than one hundred pages of motion papers."

"Seeking what?"

"To get the injunction lifted. Pitt is putting up a three-million-dollar bond as security."

"Are you ready for the hearing?"

Milton winces and shakes his head. "I'm off the case."

"What? You won the first round for them. Why off?"

"My brother's situation. The firm has put me on paid leave until his case is over. They're not real keen on their lawyers getting involved in a criminal defense matter."

"Ach, those wimps. That's pathetic. Well, Miltie, if you need a place to hang your hat until your leave is over, I have an empty office down the hall. You're welcome to it."

"Thanks, Herschel. That is quite kind of you."

"Kind shmind—you're married to my favorite niece. It's the least I can do."

Herschel opens the humidor on his desk and looks over at Milton. "A cigar?"

"No, thanks."

Milton watches as Herschel snips off the end of the cigar, slides the ashtray in front of him, lights a match, uses it to light the cigar, and take a puff.

"So, Miltie, tell me about your little brother. The case against him. I've been so busy I haven't kept up with news."

Milton tells him what he knows so far.

Herschel leans back in his chair, cigar in his mouth, and shakes his head. "Oy, your brother. That is some bad evidence."

"That's why I need a good investigator. The detective on the case agreed to let me see the motel room tomorrow. If we find a clue out there, I don't want some prosecutor to suggest that I planted it."

"And what makes you think there's a clue out there?"

"Because I know a few things about the killer already: he's a pervert and he's stupid."

"Stupid? Well, let's face it: your brother is not exactly an Oxford don. But you say also a pervert? How do you know that?"

"He apparently masturbated onto her, or maybe he got her to give him a blow-job, and then after he shot her he put out his cigarette on one of her breasts."

Herschel raised his eyebrows and nodded. "*Oy gevalt.* I'd call that compelling evidence of perversion."

"And he left that cigarette ash on her stomach. That makes him stupid. If he's stupid enough to leave a clue literally on his victim, he's stupid enough to leave some other clue out there."

An hour later, Milton and his brother, Hal, are in the small attorney-client room at the St. Louis County Jail.

"I'm going out there tomorrow," Milton says.

Hal nods dully, looking down at the table.

"You've got to try to remember everything, Hal. Keep searching your memory. Something helpful is going to pop up."

Hal looks up at his brother. "You know the worst part?"

"What?"

"To have her treat me like a moron. To use me like that."

"*This* is the worst part, Hal. Forget about that woman.

"She set me up, Bro. No, even worse, she had me set myself up." He shakes his head. "What a schmuck."

"She's dead, Hal, and you should be glad. I sure am. She was going to kill you on Friday, whether he transferred the money or not. She planted those clues to make you look like the kidnapper. That way she could claim self-defense when she shot you. If someone hadn't killed her, she would have killed you."

Hal sighs. "Still."

"Here's our problem. She's dead, but her evidence isn't. That evidence put you in jail, and we're going to have to overcome that evidence to win. Her killer got into her room without having to force the lock. Who was he? Maybe she had a partner who double-crossed her. Whatever, you may have seen a piece of that evidence without realizing it. You've got to try to remember everything.

Hal shrugs. "Okay."

Milton studies his brother. "I know it's tough, Hal. I'm going to try to get you out of here. I have that bail hearing on Friday. It's an uphill battle, but I promise I'll give it my all."

"Thanks, Milton." There are tears in Hal's eyes. "You are so awesome."

Despite himself, Milton smiles

Chapter Twenty-eight

The mood is somber this morning inside the chambers of the Honorable Roy L. Stubbs, United States District Judge for the Eastern District of Missouri. As His Honor slowly leafs through the stack of motion papers, his court clerk, Rahsan Abdullah Ahmed, and his law clerk, Norman Feigelberg, sit quietly on chairs facing the desk.

Judge Stubbs looks up from the papers. "It doesn't make sense, Rahsan." He shakes his head. "He could have told us about the kidnapping—about the ransom note."

Rahsan says nothing.

"According the newspaper," Norman says, "Mr. Pitt was afraid she'd be killed if he told anyone."

"She was killed anyway." Judge Stubbs gestures toward the motion papers. "And now this. A three-million-dollar bond as security to vacate the injunction. I suppose I should grant it. What about this other motion?" He lifts up the court papers. "The class action motion. Who are the members of that class?"

"Leonard Pitt's clients," Norman says. "The ones he ripped off with those fake checks."

"And the motion? It seeks to consolidate the class

action case with the original case. Is that something I can do?"

"I read the court decisions she cites," Norman says. "It's all good law. You could grant it—or, if you want, you could defer a ruling until Judge Weinstock gets back from vacation. It's his case, after all."

The judge places that motion on top of the other court filings, stares at the pile, and then takes a deep breath.

"Okay." He pushed back from the desk. "Let's roll."

All three stand. Norman is first out the door. Rahsan lingers by the door as the judge dons his black robe.

"You okay, Judge?"

"I suppose." Judge Stubbs buttons up his robe. "I just keep wondering, Rahsan, asking myself whether we got played here. I've tried to run the traps on this one, but it doesn't make sense. What do you think?"

Rahsan studies his judge. After a moment, he says, "Based on the law and the evidence, Yo' Honor, you done the right thing. No one can blame you for anything but doing what you been appointed to do, which is to do justice based on the law and the facts, and you done just that here."

Judge Stubbs sighs. "Yeah, maybe."

As Rahsan steps into the reception area, Norman is waiting with a big grin.

Rahsan sighs and shakes his head. "Now what?"

"The class action lawyer is out in the courtroom. Have you seen her?"

"No. Why?"

"Oh, my God. That girl is hot, Rahsan."

"You talkin' 'bout Ms. Rachel Gold?"

"You betcha."

"First off, Norman. She ain't no girl. That lady is a woman. Second off, Norman, Rachel Gold 'bout as smart and tough as they come—probably smarter and tougher than them fancy Chicago lawyers Pitt brought into this case. So my advice to you is don't even be thinking of messin' with her. She about ten levels above your pay grade."

• • ● • •

The front half of the hearing goes about as expected. Pitt's new lawyers present their motion to lift the injunction, speak movingly of their client's grief as he prepares to bury his beloved wife, and hand Rahsan the three-million-dollar bond their client has put up as security for the insurance company's claims.

Lawrence Armstrong, the Abbott & Windsor senior partner standing in for Milton Bernstein, folds his arms over his stomach, tries to make a sad face, offers his sympathies to Mr. Pitt, and tells the judge this his client has agreed to the posting of the bond in lieu of the injunction.

Judge Stubbs nods, grants the motion, and asks his court clerk to call the next case, which is the class action filed against Mid-Continent Casualty Insurance Company and Leonard Pitt's law firm.

As Rachel Gold steps to the podium, we appreciate Norman Feigelberg's rapture. She is tall and slender and beautiful, with dark curly hair and striking Mediterranean features. Her elegant black pantsuit and low heels highlight her athletic figure. She states her name for the record and briefly describes her motion. Her clients comprise the class of former clients of Leonard Pitt who were tricked into settling their claims for thousands of dollars less than the insurance company had agreed to pay in settlement.

When she finishes, Judge Stubbs turns first to the new lawyers for Leonard Pitt. "Any objection, Counselors?"

The three attorneys briefly confer, and then the lead attorney steps back to the podium. "No objection, Your Honor."

Judge Stubbs turns to Lawrence Armstrong. "What about you, Mr. Armstrong? What is the position of Mid-Continent Casualty Insurance Company?"

Armstrong looks over Rachel Gold and shakes his head, doing his best to channel a disappointed middle school principal. "Judge, my client most certainly objects to this greedy and unprecedented intrusion into its case. This is *our* claim against Mr. Pitt. We are the plaintiff here. If Miss Gold had simply sued Mr. Pitt, we might have been able to abide by consolidation as long she understood that she and her clients needed to get in line *behind* us. We were here first. But Miss Gold has sued not only Mr. Pitt but my client as well. I am, to put it mildly, shocked. Shocked. There is no justification for bringing any claim against Mid-Continent Casualty. We are the victim of this outrageous fraud, not the perpetrator. If Miss Gold wants to scurry back to her office and revise her lawsuit to delete my client, then perhaps we'd have something to talk about. But until then, there's no excuse for this bold money grab."

Judge Stubbs purses his lips in thought, looks down at the motion papers, and then turns to Rachel Gold. "Counselor, do you wish to respond?"

Rachel Gold smiles, unruffled. "I do, Your Honor. While I appreciate Mr. Armstrong's effort to make us all shed crocodile tears for his sad little multi-billion-dollar insurance company, I remind the Court—and Mr. Armstrong—that *every single settlement check* his client wrote to Mr. Pitt was for an amount that his client had deemed, after its own due diligence, to be a reasonable and proper settlement amount. If Mr. Pitt hadn't defrauded my clients by misrepresenting to them the actual amounts of those settlement checks, none of us would be here today. But, as we have learned, Mr. Pitt took those settlement checks—checks in amounts that the insurance company was comfortable writing—and skimmed off some of that money for himself. My clients, Your Honor, are the real victims here. The *only* victims. They are owed thousands and thousands of dollars, while Mid-Continent is not owed a penny. Zero. And, frankly, if Mr. Armstrong's insurance company had acted with more due diligence early on, it would have uncovered this scam years ago and thus prevented this harm to my clients. But as a direct result of the insurance company's complacency, my clients were damaged. And that, Your Honor, is why we named Mid-Continent as a defendant in our case, and that, Your Honor, is also why these two cases need to be consolidated. Thank you, Judge."

She steps back from the podium and nods at Lawrence Armstrong, whose face has turned beet red.

Judge Stubbs leans back in his chair, gavel in hand, and glances over at Rahsan, whose face remains expressionless, at least to the rest of us. After a pause, Judge Stubbs leans forward, bangs his gavel, and announces. "Ms. Gold's motion is granted. That will be all. Court is in recess."

And Rahsan commands, "All rise!"

Stage 3:
The Leg Lift

Chapter Twenty-nine

Up on the second-floor landing of the Sleepy Time Motel a uniformed cop is seated on a metal chair outside Room 205. Strips of yellow Crime Scene tape form an uneven "X" on the door. The cop stands as Milton Bernstein and Fred Butz approach.

Butz is an unimposing fellow in his sixties—more CPA than former FBI. Skinny, average height, gray crew cut, thick wire-rim glasses, white short-sleeved dress shirt, thin black tie, tan slacks belted high on the waist, thick-soled brown shoes. He is lugging a large black briefcase.

The cop turns toward Milton. "You Bernstein's lawyer?"

"That is, indeed, correct. This is Mr. Butz, my investigator."

The cop raps on the door. "They're here, Detective."

Bernie Moran opens the door. He hasn't shaved since yesterday.

He nods at Milton. "Counselor."

He turns toward Butz. "How's it hanging, Freddie?"

Butz gives Moran a thin smile. "Hello, Bernard."

Moran gestures toward the room. "Come on in, boys."

They follow Moran into the motel room.

The final position of the body is outlined in white tape on the bare mattress. The head and neck portion of the outline are stained reddish-brown.

Twenty minutes later, Milton is leaning against the wall and checking his e-mails on his cell phone. Butz is on his hands and knees, moving slowly around the room with a penlight, a pair of tweezers and a magnifying glass. He stops, picks something up with the tweezers, drops it in a specimen jar, and moves on. There are little jars on the carpet all around the room.

Moran walks out of the bathroom. "Our guy says she was shot by the bed and then dragged onto it to die."

Butz looks up with a frown. "She was kneeling when she was shot."

A few moments later, Butz is on his knees peering under the nightstand with his penlight. Milton comes over and kneels beside him.

"What is it?" he asks.

Butz is under the nightstand brushing something into his specimen jar. "I'm not sure."

He backs out, holds the jar up, and shines the light on it. Moran joins them as well. Inside the jar are a dozen or so white particles, including a couple little curlicues.

"What the fuck?" Moran says.

"Wallboard," Butz replies.

All three of them look at the wall.

"What the fuck?" Moran says.

Butz points to a spot about eye level above the night-stand. There is a small piece of white tape on the wall, almost but not quite the same color as the wall.

Moran slips on a latex glove, grasps the tape at the corner, and peels it off, revealing a neat round hole.

He snorts and shakes his head. "A peeping Tom. These fucking hot-sheets motels."

Moran hands the tape to Butz, who takes it with the tweezers and drops it into a specimen jar.

"I'll want that marked, Fred," he says.

Milton holds the jar up to the light. "These shavings look fresh."

He turns to Moran. "Who's been in the next room?"

"Let's find out."

Five minutes later, Moran is back with a room key. Milton and Butz follow him to the room next door, Number 206. He opens door and enters, followed by Milton and Butz. All eyes move to the right.

"Bingo," Moran says.

There is a hole in the wall next to the mirror. They scan the room. The only evidence of prior occupancy is the slightly rumpled bedspread.

Moran walks over to the drill hole and peers through. He turns to the other two and shakes his head. "Fucking Peeping Tom."

"Let me see," Milton says. He peers through the hole. Part of Cherry's room is visible through the hole, including the bottom half of the bed and the outline of her body.

He turns toward Butz. "Have a look."

A few minutes later, Moran and Milton are standing by the open door of Room 206. Butz moves slowly around the room on his hands and knees.

Milton says, "But your cop said no one's come in or out of this room."

"Guy could be spooked."

"If it's a guy."

Moran snorts. "True. That old broad at the front desk—Osama Bin Laden could have been living in one of these rooms and she'd have no fucking idea."

"Hmm," Butz says.

Moran and Milton turn. Butz is on his knees on the carpet below the drill hole. With one hand, he's placing a small ruler on the carpet next to a little gray object while in the other hand he holds his iPhone, focusing on that object.

Milton bends over Butz, who has just clicked the iPhone camera. Milton squints. He can see a faint dusting of gray particles on the tan carpet, but the ruler is set next to something tube-shaped, maybe a half-inch long and a quarter-inch in diameter

Butz clicks the camera. And again. And one more time. Then he sets down the iPhone, removes another evidence jar, opens it, brushes the particles inside, closes it, and scribbles something on the label.

"More wallboard, Freddie?" Moran asks.

Butz shakes his head. "Cigarette ash, I believe."

Chapter Thirty

Peggy Bernstein is seated cross-legged on the couch in the den, sipping from a mug of hot herbal tea.

Milton faces her on the loveseat across the coffee table. He's taken off his suit jacket but otherwise is still dressed for the office—white dress shirt, red bow tie, gray suit pants, black wingtips.

"I read the full police report," he says.

"And?"

"Nothing good. The bullet matches the gun stolen from the house. They have Hal's fingerprints all over the motel room."

"What do the cops say about the drywall shavings?

"The motel hasn't had a full-time chambermaid for more than month. The gal at the front desk does a cursory cleanup after a guest checks out. She hasn't vacuumed any of the rooms for at least a week."

"Who was in that room?"

"She doesn't know. She thinks someone checked in around the same time that another man checked into Room 205. That was Hal."

"She identified Hal?"

Milton shakes his head. "No. She doesn't remember what either person looked like—or so she claims. I know it was Hal for Room 205 because Hal told me. But there's no record for who was in the room next door. Actually, there's no record for either room beyond the cash payment in advance."

"How can that be?"

"Detective Moran says it's standard for those motels."

"What do you mean?"

"The ones that rent the rooms by the hour or provide temporary lodging to drug dealers and other lowlifes. Most of their guests don't want to be recognized, and management plays along."

Peggy takes another sip of tea. "What else did you find out?"

"According to the police report, Ms. Pitt was kidnapped on a Tuesday. Pitt didn't report it until Thursday. After the court froze his assets."

"Why then?"

"He claims he was trying to raise the ransom money on his own and panicked when the judge entered the injunction."

Peggy rolls her eyes. "That's convenient."

"True, but the bank records seem to back him up. At least one of the banks was in the process of clearing a one-million-dollar line of credit for a wire transfer when the injunction hit."

"When did he call the FBI?"

"Actually, he called the cops. They got into some sort of turf battle with the FBI on Friday morning. By the time the FBI got a government lawyer over to court to lift the injunction, it was too late."

"Whose Swiss bank account was it?

"The FBI has made a request through the Swiss Embassy for the identity of the account holder. Problem is the Swiss government tends to sit on those requests."

Peggy shakes her head. "Hal may not be the brightest guy in the world, Milton, but how can they believe he'd leave those magazines in his apartment or make that call to the Swiss bank from his own cell phone or buy that duct tape with his credit card if he really was the kidnapper? It's too pat."

"I agree. No one's that dumb, not even my brother."

"What about that Detective Moran? Isn't he suspicious?"

Milton frowns. "He doesn't seem to be. Then again, I should imagine he has dozens and dozens of unsolved homicide files. As far as he's concerned, this one's solved and cleared. He's moving on."

"What about that semen from her mouth? It's not even Hal's blood type?"

"I was hoping that would be our ace card. Apparently not, according to Moran and the prosecutor."

"How can that be?"

"First off, apparently the blood type of semen doesn't always match the same man's blood type of his blood."

"Really?"

"I checked it out. It's true. That's why investigators rely on DNA."

"And?"

"They're waiting for the results, but they're not optimistic."

"Why not?"

"According to the police lab technician, they didn't find any sperm in the traces of semen they were able to collect from her mouth."

"What?"

"It could mean the semen was from someone who'd had a vasectomy or that the trace amounts they collected had degraded. But it doesn't seem to bother them."

"Why not?"

"Worst case for them, according to Moran, Hal planted the evidence."

"Planted? How do you plant someone else's semen?"

"Apparently it happens. It's not that hard to find used condoms. Especially out there. I saw two in the parking lot. Gross."

"How do they think Hal even would know that?"

"They don't care, Peggy. They'll put some detective on the stand as an expert and he'll testify that this sort of thing happens."

"Are they still going to do a DNA analysis of the semen?"

"They will if they can get any DNA, but unless it points to someone in the system, they won't pursue it."

"Why not?"

"They're pretty sure they have lots of Hal's DNA in that motel room. That puts him in there. That's all the evidence they claim they need."

"What about that cigarette ash? Hal doesn't smoke."

"That's just his word. No way to prove it."

Peggy sighs. "Your brother was the perfect fall guy."

Milton says nothing.

"She was going to shoot him, wasn't she? Even if she didn't get the money."

Milton nods. "She'd make it look like she somehow got untied, shot him, and escaped."

Peggy takes a sip of tea. "So what do you think really happened at that motel?"

Milton shrugs. "That's what I keep asking myself. All we know is that her husband didn't pull the trigger. He has an airtight alibi: he was with two FBI agents in their office on Market Street when she was killed."

Peggy shakes her head. "Poor Hal."

Milton looks down at the carpet and sighs.

"What?" Peggy asks.

"My lawsuit. It put him in jail."

"No, it didn't, Milton. Your lawsuit saved his life."

"Whatever."

"Seriously, if her husband had transferred the money, she would have shot Hal in the motel room."

"All well and good, Peggy, but someone shot her, and now my little brother is in jail."

"Speaking of that lawsuit, what's going on?"

"Armstrong went over to court today. Not me, though. The firm doesn't want me anywhere near that case anymore."

"It's not your fault."

"I know. But those are my orders. The firm put me on paid leave until Hal's case is over."

"Paid leave? Why?"

Milton shrugs. "They say the case is a distraction for the firm and its clients."

"I don't understand."

"It's a corporate law firm. We don't do criminal law. Especially violent crimes."

"That's ridiculous." Peggy sets down her mug of tea on the coffee table. "You're a lawyer, Milton. You're doing exactly what a lawyer does."

"But not what an Abbott & Windsor lawyer does."

"Where will you work?"

"I'm not sure, yet. Your uncle was kind enough to offer me space in his office. I might take him up on it."

"Oy, you and Uncle Heschie. What a pair. So what happened in court today?"

Milton shakes his head. "Sam Budgah—his first lawyer—he's gone."

"What does that mean?"

"He's been terminated. Didn't even show up in court. I talked to Janet Perry this afternoon. She's the associate on the case. She told me that Pitt has new lawyers. A bunch of heavy-hitters from Warren and London, including a former U.S. Attorney from their Chicago office. He announced that his client was at home in shock, mourning the death of his wife. He told the judge that if the injunction remained in effect, it would close down the Pitt's office, put a dozen people out of work, jeopardize the rights of the hundreds and hundreds of clients of the firm."

"Oh, my God. Are you kidding?"

Milton forces a smile. "He must have sensed he was losing the judge there, so he played his trump card. He offered to post a three-million-dollar bond if the injunction were dissolved. That way our insurance company client could prosecute its damages claim without any prejudice and his poor grieving client could bury his dead wife."

"The judge went along with that?"

Milton nods. "Bond was posted at five o'clock this afternoon. Pitt's free again to prey on the public."

"That's disgusting."

"That's the law."

Milton chuckles.

"What?" Peggy asks.

"Armstrong is not happy."

"Why not? A three-million-dollar bond is pretty good security."

"He liked being the plaintiff. Now he's a defendant, too."

"What do you mean?"

"A class action got filed against Pitt and Mid-Continent Casualty."

"A class action? Of who?"

"All of the clients that Pitt defrauded. And worse yet, the judge consolidated the class action with our case today. Janet said Armstrong was furious when he got back to the office. Screaming and yelling." Milton looks up with raised eyebrows. "Guess who's representing that class?"

"Who?"

"The one and only Rachel Gold."

"I know Rachel. We're both volunteers at the Jewish Food Pantry. She's awesome. Wait—she used to be at your firm, right?"

"In the Chicago office. She left a few years back and then moved to St. Louis. She has her own practice now."

"Wow. So she's on the other side, eh?"

"Yep, and Armstrong is one unhappy camper."

"He's a big boy. He can deal with it."

Milton looks down at the carpet. After a moment, he says, "Speaking of bonds."

Peggy frowns. "Yes?"

"I called my mom this afternoon."

"Down in Florida?"

Milton nods.

"Called her about what?"

"About helping post a bond."

"What bond?"

"For Hal."

"What do you mean?"

"There's a hearing tomorrow. On my motion for bail for Hal."

"For Hal? Do judges ever do that for someone held on murder charges?"

"Sometimes. He's not a flight risk. It's not his semen. I've got some points to argue. I found a few cases. It could happen."

"But?"

Milton shrugs. "It won't be cheap."

Milton's cell phone rings. He pulls it out of his shirt pocket, squints at the caller ID, and stands up. "It's my expert," he says to Peggy. "I have to take this."

He puts the phone to his ear and he starts toward the front hall. "Fred?"

The conversation lasts a few minute, mostly Milton listening and saying an occasional *Okay*.

"Thanks, Fred," Milton says. "I'll call you tomorrow."

He walks back into the den.

"Well?" Peggy asks.

He takes his seat facing her. "That was Fred Butz. Your uncle is right. He's good."

"Tell me."

"Butz confirmed the drill shavings on the rug. They're drywall, same type as the walls in the motel room."

"What about the ash?"

"That's where the plot thickens. Apparently, the ash is from a cigar, not a cigarette."

"How does he know that?"

"He's good, Peggy. He said he got suspicious when examining the autopsy photos. He said that the burn mark on her breast looked larger than the profile of a typical burn mark from a cigarette. He did an analysis of the chemical composition of the ash he collected at the motel. It matches the chemical composition of various cigars manufactured by the General Cigar Company. They make White Owls, Tiparillos, Robert Burns, and a bunch of other brands. Many are made from the same mix of cigar leaf and filler. When were out at that motel, he found an intact piece of ash on the carpet in the room next door. He photographed it alongside a ruler. He says the diameter of that ash most closely matches the diameter of a Tiparillo."

"Meaning?"

Milton grins. "Ergo, our suspect smokes Tiparillos."

Peggy gives him a sympathetic smile. "It's a start, Milton."

Milton shrugs. "Barely."

"You don't have the burden of proof, right? That's what you always tell me. All you need is reasonable doubt."

Milton shakes his head. "The jury's going to need a lot more than a cigar ash and drywall shavings before they start questioning the state's evidence."

"What other options are there?"

Milton glances down. "Find the real killer."

"Find the killer? Who's going to do that?"

He looks up and shrugs. "Me?"

"My God, Milton. These people are thugs."

"True."

"And you? A nice Jewish boy from the suburbs? Are you crazy?"

Milton offers a weak smile. "I'm not going to do anything crazy, Peggy. But still."

"But still what?"

He takes a deep breath and exhales slowly. "Someone screwed up. Big-time. Hal doesn't smoke cigars. If I can trace that cigar ash back to the killer, I bet I can trace the killer back to Pitt."

"Trace the cigar ash? Do you have any idea how many people smoke those things? How are you going to do that?"

Milton shrugs. "I don't know how yet, but I swear I will. I have to, Peggy. He's my brother. My only brother."

Chapter Thirty-one

That there is even a genuine bail hearing for a defendant facing such charges is noteworthy. That the hearing is going well is even more noteworthy. Of course, everything is relative. The phrase "going well" here means that when the clerk announced, "State of Missouri versus Harold S. Bernstein, Defendant's Motion for Release on Bond," the presiding judge did not simply bang down his gavel and declare, "Denied! Next case."

Instead, Milton stepped to the podium to enter his appearance as counsel for defendant. He was followed by an assistant prosecutor named Melinda Schimmel entering her appearance for the State of Missouri. Staring down at them, lips pursed, eyes squinting, is the Honorable Dick McCarthy.

Judge McCarthy is a formidable jurist in every sense of the word, including physical. He stands at least six-foot-six and weighs at least three hundred pounds. The high-backed leather chair behind his judicial bench audibly groans whenever he lowers his bulk into it. He has a thick shock of white hair on top, a pair of large protruding ears, a bulbous red nose, and a deep foghorn of a voice that reverberates throughout the courtroom

"Counsel?" Judge McCarthy says, staring down at Milton, "Your client is Hal Bernstein?"

"Yes, Your Honor. And I am here today—"

"The pitcher?"

"Uh, yes. Not anymore, though."

Judge McCarthy gestures toward the defendant, who is seated at defense counsel's table in his prison-issue orange jumpsuit. "What happened?"

"He was framed, Your Honor," Milton answers, his voice rising in genuine outrage. "I can assure this Honorable Court that we intend to—"

"—I'm not referring to this case, Counsel. I am referring to your client's baseball career. He was one of the finest pitchers Mizzou ever had. I saw him pitch twice down there. That boy had remarkable control. What happened?"

Milton stares at the judge, eyes blinking behind his thick lenses. After a pause, he says, "He suffered an injury, Your Honor. In a motor vehicle accident. Unfortunately, it ended his baseball career prematurely."

"Damn shame." The judge looks over at Hal and shakes his head. "Could have made it to the big-time, son."

Hal lowers his head.

Judge McCarthy turns back to Milton with a disapproving frown. "So instead of pitching for the Cardinals—or preferably, for the Cubs, if I can disclose such a controversial allegiance in this courtroom—so instead of pitching, he kidnaps and kills the wife of a prominent attorney?"

"Precisely," the assistant prosecutor says.

"Precisely not," Milton snaps. "We will have our day in court, as guaranteed by our Constitution, Your

Honor, and I can guarantee Ms. Schimmel that we will prove beyond a shadow of a doubt my client's innocence. We will demonstrate in open court that Harold Bernstein was framed. He is just another victim, albeit one who's still alive. And that is precisely why I am here today, Your Honor."

"Nevertheless, Counsel," Judge McCarthy says, eyebrows raised, "your client is charged with a capital offense. Actually, two capital offenses. We typically don't release such defendants on bond."

"This is hardly your typical case, Your Honor, and my client—who has never before been charged with any violation of the law, including even a speeding ticket or a parking ticket—whose prior record is as clean as a newborn infant's, is most assuredly not a typical defendant. As set forth in our motion papers, including the exhibits and affidavits attached there, my client—"

Milton is on a roll, and when Milton is on a roll you just have to sit back and let him roll, even if you're Judge Dick McCarthy.

As always, Milton has done his homework. While he did miss the significance of the University of Missouri connection—where Dick McCarthy not only earned his bachelor's and law degrees but played varsity baseball himself, served one term as chair of the MU Alumni Association, and drives a Chrysler 300 that is custom painted in Mizzou's black-and-gold colors—Milton has amassed a trove of data on the judge's prior bail rulings in capital cases, and he has read everything he could find on the saga of the judge's nephew, Lex O'Connor, who was held without bail on rape charges and eventually exonerated after spending close to a year in prison awaiting trial.

And thus, after highlighting the evidentiary issues— including the Tiparillo burn on the victim and the apparent third-party semen deposit in her mouth— Milton moves on to the qualities his younger brother shares with the judge's nephew—without, of course, ever mentioning that nephew. Those qualities include: no flight risk, no prior record, no danger to the community, and close family ties in the area (which, for Hal, is a brother, a sister-in-law, and two beloved nieces). Even better than Lex O'Conner, who was a college student at the time, Hal not only has a steady job (well, maybe that's a stretch, but Milton has attached as Exhibit 34 a letter of recommendation from Hal's boss) but a job that involves...drum roll...SAVING LIVES!!

"And last but certainly not least, Your Honor, the defendant is my little brother. He is family. He will live at my house through the trial. I will be responsible for him at all times, and I will accept whatever obligation this Court deems fair and just for that responsibility."

Chapter Thirty-two

Three hours later, Milton steps into the foyer of his home.

"Milton?" Peggy calls from the kitchen.

He sets down his briefcase in the front hall and heads toward the kitchen, where Peggy is at the island cutting up salad greens

"Well?" she asks.

"I have good news and some sort-of good news."

"Tell me the sort-of first."

Milton forces a smile. "You'll be seeing more of me for the next few months."

"What does that mean?"

"I moved in to your uncle's office after court today. But since I only have one case, maybe I'll be able to get home for dinner most nights."

"That's good. But Uncle Heschie…" Peggy shakes her head sadly. "Oh, Milton."

"It's okay, Peg. It's only temporary. I'll be fine. And when the case is over, I'll be back at Abbott & Windsor."

"So tell me the good news."

"The judge granted my motion. He's going to release Hal."

"Oh, my God!" She comes around the island and gives Milton a hug, tears in her eyes. "My hero! That's wonderful, honey."

"It certainly is." He pauses and leans back. "There are a few conditions, of course."

Peggy's smile fades as she takes a step back. "Conditions? Such as?"

"He'll have to live with us until the trial."

She nods, thinking it over as she walks back around the island to the cutting board. "Okay. We can put him in the basement bedroom. He'll have his own bathroom down there."

"Good idea."

"When does he move in?"

Milton winces. "That brings me to the other condition."

Peggy gives him a look. "What is it?"

"In lieu of a cash bond, the Court is willing to accept a property bond in the amount of one million dollars. It's very unusual."

"What property?"

"My mother's condo in Florida and, uh, and our house."

"What does that mean?"

"The court gets a lien on the property to secure the bail. If Hal fails to appear in court, the court can foreclose on the property to obtain the bail amount."

Peggy's eyes widen. "So we could lose our house?"

"Only if Hal didn't show up for his trial. That's not going to happen, Peggy. It's Hal. He won't do that to us."

"Milton, he's facing life in prison. Maybe the death penalty. He's got a darn good reason not to show up."

"I know my brother, Peggy."

Peggy places her hands on the island and leans forward, eyebrows raised. "Milton, your brother is a moron."

"But he's a good person."

"Oh, my God, Milton."

"It'll be okay."

"When does all this craziness happen?"

"My mom needs to sign the papers, and then we do. You and me, Peggy. I can't do this alone—and I would never do this alone."

She closes her eyes. "Oy."

Chapter Thirty-three

On this sunny Saturday afternoon, scores of parked cars line the road into Resurrection Cemetery, including a fair sampling of official St. Louis and St. Louis County: police cars, fire chief cars, City Hall sedans, and several stretch limos, each with a chauffeur in gray livery, black cap, and aviator sunglasses lounging against the driver's side, arms crossed. The sounds of a Mizzou football game radio broadcast can be heard from one of the limos.

The gravesite is perched on a gentle slope overlooking the River Des Peres. Hundreds of men and women, mostly men, are gathered around the graveside tent. Leonard Pitt is seated in the center of the front row facing the open grave. The service will be starting soon.

Milton stands off to the side, about twenty yards away from the gathering. As he studies the faces in the crowd, Detective Bernie Moran walks over.

Milton nods at him. "Big crowd."

"Guy with Pitt's clout draws a big crowd.

"You still on the case?"

"Barely." Moran steps further back from the crowd,

gesturing Milton to follow. When Milton gets close, he says, "Just cleaning up some loose ends."

"Such as?"

Moran shakes his head. "Such as some loose ends, Milton."

"Such as why Pitt waited until Thursday night to call the police when his wife was supposedly kidnapped on Tuesday. Doesn't that seem a little odd?"

"Listen, pal, I see odd every fucking day. It's part of my job description."

"Such as how my brother could be at the pool when she was supposedly held captive at the motel."

"He called in sick on the day of the kidnapping, he was off the next two days, and he lit out of there on Friday afternoon like a bat out of hell."

"How did he keep her in the motel room when he was on the beach?"

"Ask your brother. He's the one who bought the duct tape. The medical examiner founds traces of the tape and abrasions on her ankles and wrists."

"That doesn't prove he tied her up."

"For chrissakes, Milton. This ain't some cop show on TV. We're not fucking CSI St. Louis. We got loose ends. Every goddamm case has loose ends—hey, you listening to me?"

But Milton has turned toward the narrow road that runs through the cemetery grounds. A black Mustang had pulled up on the grass behind the empty hearse. The driver, a bulky man in his forties dressed in a black suit, white shirt, and skinny black tie, walks past them toward the crowd at the gravesite.

"Who is that?" Milton asks.

"A piece of shit," Moran says. "Ex-copper named Bledsoe. Billy Bledsoe."

Milton waits until Bledsoe disappears into the crowd around the tent, and then starts toward the Mustang. Curious, Moran follows.

Milton glances back. "Ex?"

"Yeah. Shot two fags in a Tower Grove Park men's room. Got his ass kicked off the force."

"What's he do these days?"

"Heard he works for Pitt. Probably one of his chasers."

They have reached the driver's side of the car.

Milton turns to face Moran, eyebrows raised. "Works for Pitt?"

"So I hear. Why do you care?"

Milton points at the grass. "Recognize that?"

Moran stares. "That was Bledsoe's?"

"I saw him stub it out when he got out of the car."

"Okay. So?"

"Fred Butz identified that ash on the carpet in the room next door. It wasn't cigarette ash. It was cigar ash. And guess what type of cigar?" He points down. "That one."

"A Tiparillo?"

"Yep."

Moran kneels down and pulls an envelope out of the inside pocket of his jacket. "Interesting."

Moran uses the end of the pen to carefully push the crushed Tiparillo into the envelope.

Ten minutes later, Milton is standing by his car, cell phone to his ear. The cemetery grounds are visible in the background.

"First name Billy," Milton says. "Maybe William."

"Okay," Butz replies. "Last name is spelled B-L-E-D-S-O-E?"

"I think so. Moran didn't spell it for me."

"I'll see what I can find out."

"I'll come by your office later this afternoon."

"Okay."

Chapter Thirty-four

Milton takes the call down the hall from Herschel Goldman's office, inside the small conference room he now uses as his temporary office. When he finishes his telephone conversation with Fred Butz, he walks back over to Herschel's office and waits in the doorway as Herschel finishes what sounds like a conversation with opposing counsel.

"So think about it, Bob," Herschel says into the phone. "My client is a mensch. A reasonable man looking for nothing more than fair compensation for his injuries and his loss of income. If the insurance company wants to resolve this in a just and prompt manner, you know my number. If not, my friend, I will see you in court next Monday."

He hangs up, smiles at Milton, and shakes his head, gesturing toward the phone. "Oy, a real putz, he is. And not too *klieg*, either. Don't get me started. Come on in. Have a seat, *boychik*. *Nu*? So what did you learn about *Señor* Tiparillo?"

"He's a creep."

"Oh?"

"And dangerous. Full name: William E. Bledsoe, Jr. He was a boxer in Joliet back in the nineties. Fought under the name Billy the Kid. According to Fred Butz, Bledsoe was strictly a club fighter, whatever that means. Joined the St. Louis police force in 2007, whereupon he distinguished himself and his profession by two separate shootings in the space of one month. Both times at night in a Tower Grove Park restroom. Both victims were unarmed homosexual males. Both shot in the genitalia."

"My God! In the balls?"

"Worse. One in the left testicle, the other in the penis."

Herschel grimaces. "Oy, vey."

"And guess who represented Bledsoe in the civil lawsuits filed by the families?"

"Leonard Pitt?"

"Yep. Apparently as a favor to someone in City Hall. Bledsoe has worked for Pitt ever since."

"Doing what?"

"Fred couldn't pin that down. He does some work as a chaser and some as a driver for Pitt and some as just a gopher."

Herschel nods and twirls his mustache. "Okay? And this tells you?"

"That Bledsoe killed her."

"Really?" Herschel leans back in his chair and frowns. "Why?"

"On Pitt's orders."

"Again, Miltie, why?"

Milton sits down in the chair facing his uncle. "According to Hal, Pitt and Cherry had a terrible marriage. Maybe Pitt was looking to get something on her, maybe grounds for an annulment. After all, the guy is a Catholic now. Thus he cannot get a divorce. Or maybe Pitt was just suspicious, wanted to find out what his wife does all day. With Bledsoe around, he didn't need to hire a private eye to see what she was up to."

"Okay. And?"

"Here's my theory. Pitt has Bledsoe tail her for a few weeks. He sees my brother leave with Cherry on the day of the so-called kidnapping. He follows them to the motel and reports back to his boss. Thus when Pitt finds the ransom note, he knows it's a sham. And by then, the lawsuit we filed is a week old."

"The one where the judge froze his assets?"

"Exactly." Milton shakes his head. "Like an answer to his prayers. That's why Pitt hired that buffoon Sam Budgah and had him file that motion for an emergency hearing. If the judge freezes his assets, he has the perfect excuse for not transferring the money. And when he doesn't pay the ransom, the supposed kidnapper kills her."

"This Bledsoe character? He's the shooter?"

"Makes sense, doesn't it, Heschie? The puzzle pieces fit. Bledsoe keeps an eye on her through that hole he drills in the motel room wall. Pitt instructs Bledsoe to kill her on Friday, as soon as the ransom deadline expires."

"Can you place Bledsoe in that other room?"

"All I have so far is that cigar ash."

"Who rented the room?"

"They don't know."

"How can that be?"

"I looked at the police file yesterday. Someone called—

a woman, the night manager thinks—and reserved that motel room for a week. Specified Room 206."

"Name?"

Milton smiles. "Jane Doe."

"You're kidding me."

"It happens, according to the manager. She wasn't their first Jane Doe. As long as they pay cash in advance, they're okay with it."

Herschel chuckles. "A regular hot-sheets motel, eh?"

"I guess so."

"Did they tell you what she looks like?"

"No. According to the police report, the night manager said that a messenger service dropped off the cash and picked up the room key."

"Which messenger service?"

Milton shakes his head. "He didn't know. Some guy. He wasn't wearing a messenger uniform."

Herschel leans back in his chair and twirls his mustache as he mulls it over. "Fingerprints?"

"Nope. I'm sure he wiped them off before he left. According to the police report, the doorknobs were clean. So were the bathroom faucets, the toilet seat, the phone." Milton pauses, his eyebrows raised. "The phone. Damn. The phone."

"What phone?"

"In the motel room."

"You mean the land line?"

Milton grins. "Exactly."

"You don't think he has a cell phone?"

"I'm sure he does. But he probably didn't use it."

"Why not?"

"I assume his cell phone has geo-tracking. I think they all do. If he made a call from his cell phone in that room, there'd be a record of it with the cell phone company.

"Okay. So what's so interesting about that phone in the room?"

"Maybe nothing. But…"—Milton stands—"no harm checking."

"Checking what? Where are you going, Miltie?"

"I need to run something down. I'll tell you what I find out."

Chapter Thirty-five

We're back in the front office of the Sleepy Time Motel. The clock on the wall shows six-ten p.m. Milton is talking with the female manager. He has a clipboard in his hands and a pencil behind his ear.

"Really?" Milton says.

"Oh, yes." She smiles. "My boss is real pleased. Guess you folks don't hear that too often, eh?"

Milton nods and grins. "We are truly delighted, ma'am, and we want to keep it that way. That's why we do these free spot checks. We check your list against ours to make sure you're picking up all those calls. Making sure they'll all show up on your guests' bill. It can be a nice profit center for folks like you, as I'm sure your boss will agree."

He pauses to check his "notes."

"Let me see," he says. "Sleepy Time Motel. Can I take a quick peek at the phone logs for, let me see, ah, yes, for the Thursday and Friday two weeks ago? That would be the tenth and eleventh of September."

"Wait right here."

She goes into the back office and returns a moment later with a photocopy of several pages of telephone phone logs.

"Here you go." She hands him the documents. "This is for all of that week, but it's divided by day so you'll be able to check those dates you mentioned."

"Thank you, ma'am."

"Boy, it's been a real circus out here."

"Really? How come?"

"That poor little gal got killed on that Friday. The fourth. Talk about a shock."

"Good lord!" Milton raises his eyebrows and opens in his mouth. "I didn't realize it happened here. I read all about it. That's terrible."

"They had me on Channel Two, you know?"

"No kidding?" Milton smiles. "A real celebrity, huh?"

"You betcha." She gives him a wink. "Behave and I might just give you an autograph."

"Oh, my! I will behave. I promise, ma'am."

She laughs.

Milton says, "Well, Thanks again, ma'am. We'll compare it to our records. If you're not catching all the calls, we will send someone out here next week to adjust the system."

Milton gets in his car, pulls out of the motel parking lot, and drives about a mile down the road, where he turns into the parking lot of a 7-Eleven, parks, shuts off the engine, and reaches for the telephone log.

There were no phone calls from Room 205, which is the room where Cherry's body was found. There are, however, two calls from Room 206, and both to the same telephone number, one on Thursday afternoon at 5:37 p.m. and one on Friday morning at 9:43 a.m. Milton circles the phone numbers, takes out his cell phone, starts to dial, and then pauses. He scans the parking lot. There is a pay phone along the walkway to the left of the entrance to the 7-Eleven.

He walks over to the pay phone, lifts the receiver, drops in two quarters, glances down at the printout, and dials the number on the telephone log for Room 206

The sound of the phone ringing. Once…twice… three times.

And then a click. And a pause. And then a woman's voice: "You have reached the law offices of Leonard Pitt & Associates. We are sorry no one is here to answer your call, but our offices are closed for the day. Your call is very important to us. At the sound of the tone, please leave your name and telephone number and someone will call you during our regular office hours. Thank you."

Beep.

Click.

Milton hangs up the phone, turns toward the parking lot, clenches his fist over his head, and starts softly chanting, "Attica! Attica! Attica!"

Stage 4:
The Stride

Chapter Thirty-six

Milton stands next to Peggy at the kitchen window as they peer out into the backyard. Both are smiling.

"I must confess," Peggy says. "Your brother is cute. And sweet. Our girls adore him."

Sara and Maddy both have on their princess outfits, complete with tiaras and scepters. Hal is on his hands and knees, apparently playing the role of the royal pony. Maddy rides as Sara leads him around the swing set. Hal neighs, snorts, and then whinnies. Both girls start laughing, Maddy so hard that she almost falls off Hal's back.

"He's been playing with them for the last two hours," Peggy says. "They've played house, he read them some books, and now they're doing princesses at the castle."

Milton nods. "That's nice."

Peggy turns to him. "Oh, it's wonderful, Milton." She gives him a kiss. "You have to get him out of this horrible mess."

Milton nods. "First things first. We got him out of jail. Out of jail and into our house."

Peggy smiles. "Sort of our house, right? And sort of the court's house."

Milton shrugs. "Sort of. We'll be okay. Hal is going to show up for the trial. And with any luck, maybe I get this over without a trial."

"Oh?"

"I have an idea."

"What kind of idea?"

"I'll explain it later. But you and the girls are going to have to leave town for a few days."

Peggy stepped back. "What are you talking about, Milton?"

"It'll be safer for everyone, and the girls will love spending time with your parents. I'll explain after they're in bed."

"I do not like the sound of this, Milton. Not one bit."

• • ● • •

Three hours later. The dinner dishes are washed, the girls are asleep, and Peggy is upstairs reading the new Scott Turow novel. Hal and Milton are seated side-by-side out back on the patio. Suspended above them in the clear night sky is a full moon.

Hal shakes his head. "I don't get it, Bro. It's not my DNA. Why isn't that enough?"

"That's exactly what I said to Moran. He brushed it off."

"How?"

"He said at most it might indicate you planted the semen or had an accomplice."

"I didn't have any damn accomplice. I didn't do anything. She played me, Bro. Pure and simple."

"I know, Hal. I know."

"And those phone calls to Pitt's office from that motel room? What about that?"

"He claims it doesn't prove anything. He says a guy like Pitt, who does all that advertising on TV, gets dozens and dozens of calls every day. He says it's more likely someone in that room saw one of his ads and called him."

"On two different days?"

Milton turns toward his younger brother. "Hal, they're convinced the case is a lock. Unless we can hand them a confession, they're going to just press ahead."

"Oh, Jeez." Hal lowers his head into his hands. "I'm stupid, yes. And a total sucker. I'm guilty of that, but I'm innocent, Milton. I didn't kidnap her, and I certainly didn't kill her."

Hal turns to Milton, tears in his eyes. "What can I do?"

Milton leans back and stares up at the moon. After a long pause, he lowers his head and looks at Hal. "You can hand them a confession."

Hal frowns. "From who?"

"The killer."

"A confession from the real killer?"

"Precisely."

"Are you serious?"

"I am, indeed."

"I don't understand."

Milton smiles. "Then I shall explain, little brother."

Chapter Thirty-seven

To fully understand what happens next, you need to know something about Milton that may not be readily apparent. In the biological hierarchy of the species *Homo sapiens*, there is a taxonomic subspecies known as *Nerd*. Beneath that subspecies, according to the International Code of Zoological Nomenclature, there exist many sub-units, mostly comprised of males under the age of fifty with above-average IQs and below-average athletic skills. There is the Sub-Unit *Fan Boys*, whose members often show up at Comic Con events in Star Wars costumes. Many Fan Boys own action figures (still in their original plastic containers) of various Spawn characters, fervently believe that the Great American Novel is the Neil Gaiman graphic novel *The Sandman*, and are stereotyped as still residing, at the age of thirty, in the basement bedroom of their mother's house. (Many actually have their own apartments.) And then there is the Sub-Unit known as *D & D's*, whose members gather late at night in suburban basements to play Dungeons & Dragons. And then there are, of course, the Sub-Unit *Sports Geeks*, usually of the baseball genre, who worship at the Shrine of Bill James, micro-manage their fantasy baseball and football teams, and bombard sports websites with obscure statistics and passionate riffs on BABIPs and TZs. And so on. Researchers continue to identify new sub-units.

Milton is a member of that special sub-unit of *Nerds* known as *Quote Geeks*. You want Walter Sobchak's defense of remaining Jewish after divorcing his wife? Milton can deliver it verbatim and with an impressive impersonation of John Goodman. Just listen to Milton's rendition of Walter's final riposte, after the Dude tells him that his clinging to Judaism just proves that he's "living in the fucking past":

"Three thousand years of beautiful tradition, from Moses to Sandy Koufax?! [Shouting] You're goddamn right I'm living in the fucking past!!"

Name your movie and Milton will give you the lines, delivered with all the intonations and emotions of the original. You want Alec Baldwin's "watch" speech as Blake in *Glengarry Glen Ross*? Done. Steve Martin's rental car rant as Neal Page in *Planes, Trains and Automobiles*? Done. John Belushi's Pearl Harbor pep talk as Bluto in *Animal House*? Done. Peter Finch's amusement park diatribe as Howard Beale in *Network*? Done.

Close your eyes, try to ignore the nasal voice, and you can be in Rick's Café in Casablanca, Morocco, or Michael Corleone's study in Las Vegas.

Former members of Milton's study group at the University of Chicago Law School still speak in awe of his rendition of "The Further Adventures of Nick Danger" from Side B of the Firesign Theatre 1969 album *How Can You Be in Two Places at Once When You're Not Anywhere at All*.

The ENTIRE Side B.

By heart.

One of his masterpieces is Jack Nicholson as Boston gangland chief Frank Costello in Martin Scorsese's motion picture *The Departed*. Over the phone, you'd swear it was Nicholson.

Got it? Good. Now back to the present:

Billy Bledsoe is on the couch in his living room. He's spooning cold ravioli out of a can while he watches a UFC match on TV. As he scrapes out the last chunk of ravioli the phone rings.

He glances over at the phone, irritated.

Caller ID Blocked reads the message.

After the fourth ring, he picks it up the receiver. "Yeah?"

"How much he pay you?" a gravelly voice asks.

Bledsoe frowns. "How much what?"

"For killing her. How much?"

"Who the fuck is this?"

"Your new partner."

"Who is this?"

"You got shit in your ears, Billy? How much?"

"Hey, man, what the fuck you talking about?"

"What do you think I'm talking about, Bledsoe? The price he paid you to kill his wife."

"Hey, man, you must be nuts. I don't know what you're talking about."

"Listen careful, Little Billy." A pause, and now at a slower pace: "I was at the motel. I heard the gunshot. I saw you walk out of her room. Got the license plate off your car. That black Mustang you drive. Took me a while to find you, but I did. You following me, Billy?"

"You must be fucking crazy, man. I don't know what you're talking about."

"Here's what I'm talking about, Billy. I'm talking about the fact that I got you by the short hairs. You startin' to catch on?"

Bledsoe's face is flushed, his breathing quicker. "Who are you?"

"I'm the guy who's going to go to the cops day after tomorrow and tell them what I saw at the Sleepy Time Motel last Friday around noon. Unless, of course, I find me a partner before then. And you know what that means?"

"What?"

"That means twenty-five large, partner. Before midnight tomorrow."

"Twenty-five grand?"

"The job's worth fifty. Easy. I'm assuming you're not a total douche bag and cut the price. All I want's my twenty-five. You bargained for more than fifty, good for you. Keep the extra. But if he got you for less than fifty, too bad for you. Either way, I want my twenty-five."

"Who are you?"

"Couple other things, partner. I'll call tomorrow night at seven. On the dot. To let you know where to bring the money. You can tell your boss if you want. You do, though, you better be careful. Real careful. The man's got guns and we both know he knows how to use 'em. So you be sure to tell him that killing you—no matter how tempting that might seem—ain't gonna solve *his* problem. I'll just deal direct with him. And one last thing, Billy. Listen careful. You try to fuck with me and I guarantee you'll find yourself in a world of hurt."

Click.

Bledsoe slowly hangs up and stares at the TV screen. Ten minutes pass as he sits motionless on the couch, the near-empty can of ravioli resting between his legs.

Finally, he reaches for the phone and dials.

Pitt's voice: "Hello?"

"We got a big problem, Boss."

"We?"

"Yeah."

"What kind of problem?"

"Some bastard saw me leave her room. Wants twenty-five large to keep quiet."

A long pause, and then: "Get over here now. Park in the alley. Come in the back door."

Click.

Bledsoe hangs up and just sits there. Eventually, he reaches for the remote and turns off the TV.

He stands, takes the car keys off the coffee table, heads for the door.

He pauses as his hand touches the doorknob.

That's when he recalls part of that mystery phone call: *You can tell your boss if you want. You do, though, you better be careful. Real careful. The man's got guns and we both know he knows how to use 'em.*

Bledsoe walks back to his bedroom. He reemerges carrying a Hi-Standard Longhorn handgun. He sights down the 9" barrel, slides the gun into the shoulder holster, slips on a black leather jacket, and heads out the door.

Chapter Thirty-eight

"Whoa!" Hal shakes his head in amazement. "That was awesome!"

Milton shrugs. "We shall see."

"Bro, you could like totally win an Oscar for that performance."

"First things first." Milton holds up the flip-phone. "We need to dump this."

They're seated in Milton's Chevy Impala, which Milton had parked behind the Missouri History Museum in Forest Park. That's where he'd made the call, not wanting it to be traced back to his house—an unlikely danger, given that it was one of four cheap pre-paid flip-phones he'd bought at Walmart that afternoon, thanks to a tip from Uncle Heschie, who'd represented a few drug dealers over the years.

He starts the engine, pulls out of the parking area, and drives slowly along Lagoon Drive until he reaches the Grand Basin, where he brakes and puts the car into Park. To their left is the Grand Basin, which sits at the foot of Art Hill. The eight fountains in the Basin, all brightly lit, shoot water thirty feet into the night sky. At the top of Art Hill stands the imposing bronze statue of

King Louis IX of France—Saint Louis—on horseback, sword held high, backlit by the Saint Louis Art Museum. Three couples are strolling along the classical promenade that lines the Grand Basin.

Milton opens the door and looks at Hal. "Wait here."

Hal watches as his brother walks around the front of the car to the right side of the road and through the tall grass on the unlit side of the basin, where he heaves the phone into the water. He comes back to the car, shifts into Drive, and heads toward the Forest Park exit at Skinker.

"So what's next?" Hal asks.

"I will call him tomorrow. Set up a drop point."

"You really think it'll work?"

"Maybe." Milton looks over at Hal and smiles. "They don't cover this part in law school."

Hal laughs. "You are awesome, Milton."

"We shall see."

They drive in silence until Milton turns onto the Forest Park Expressway.

He glances over at Hal. "How are you holding up?"

"I'm hanging in there."

"Good."

"Got some decent news from the Grizzlies today."

Milton looks over at him. "Oh?"

"I drove over there after work this afternoon to pitch batting practice."

The Grizzlies are the Gateway Grizzlies, a professional baseball team in the Frontier League. Their home field is across the Mississippi River in Sauget, Illinois.

"Batting practice? Isn't the baseball season over?"

"It's the Grizzlies' version of winter ball. More like fall ball. This month and part of next month."

"How did you do?" Milton asks.

"Bobbie Carson told me to throw my game stuff."

"Who's Bobbie Carson?"

"Their pitching coach. Pitched two years for the Royals."

"What does that mean? Game stuff."

"Like it's a real game."

"How did you do?"

Hal shrugs. "Not too shabby. Faced four batters. Struck 'em all out."

"That sounds promising."

"Can't throw heat anymore." Hal shakes his head. "Not since that accident. But I got some decent control again, especially with the curve and cutter. Both were working for me today. Except for a couple foul balls, those four guys never made contact."

"Contact?"

"As in getting the bat on the ball. Four strikeouts. Afterward, Bobbie told me that if I can get through this criminal stuff and come out of it in one piece, they'll have a place for me in the rotation."

Milton nods. "Good for you."

"Yeah. Sure would be nice." Hal sighs. "Been a long strange road back."

Chapter Thirty-nine

Leonard Pitt and Billy Bledsoe are seated in the den of Pitt's home. Pitt is behind his desk. Bledsoe is on the upholstered leather chair, his feet resting on the matching leather ottoman. Drapes are drawn, lights are low. Pitt is staring at the corner of the Persian rug in front of the desk, frowning. He looks up at the crinkling sound. Bledsoe is removing the wrapper from a Tiparillo.

"You can't smoke that in this house."

"Oh. Sure." Bledsoe grins and shrugs. "Sorry, Mr. Pitt."

He puts the Tiparillo back in the inside pocket of his jacket.

Pitt continues to stare at the corner of the Persian rug. Bledsoe waits.

Finally, he clears his throat. "I swear, Mr. Pitt. I didn't see no one out there."

Pitt, still staring the rug, nods. "I'll get the money tomorrow morning."

"Really? We gonna pay that guy?"

Pitt stares at Bledsoe. "Of course not."

"Oh. Okay."

Bledsoe waits. Pitt says nothing.

"So, uh, then what are we gonna do?"

"We? No, Billy. You. This is your problem, and you are going to solve it."

"Okay. Sure. Uh, how?"

"You are going to kill him."

"Yeah. I get it. Makes sense." A pause. "When?"

"At the drop point."

"Tomorrow night?"

"Yes, Billy, tomorrow night. You are first going to show him the money. Then you are going to talk to him. And then you are going to kill him."

"Maybe I should just ambush him."

"No, Billy. You will do exactly what I tell you to do. Exactly. No fuck-ups this time. You will talk to him. I want you to hear what he has to say. I want you to find out whether anyone else is involved, and, if so, who they are. No shooting until then. Understand?"

Billy frowns. "Okay. But what if someone else is involved?"

"Then we will deal with it."

"Okay. Sure."

Pitt stares at Bledsoe. He squints and then shakes his head. "Really, Billy?"

Bledsoe frowns, confused. "Really what, Mr. Pitt?"

"I hope you aren't planning to kill him with that cheap Longhorn."

Bledsoe glances down at the bulge of the shoulder holster beneath his jacket. "Uh, I hadn't decided."

"Is it registered?"

Billy smiles. "Yep. It's perfectly legal, Mr. Pitt."

Pitt shakes his head. "Billy, sometimes I wonder if you can possibly be as stupid as you seem. You don't kill a man with a registered gun."

Pitt walks out of the room and returns a moment later with a Walther Model P-38 and a handful of bullets. He holds them out to Bledsoe.

"Here. This gun's clean. Give me the Longhorn."

Billy reluctantly makes the switch.

Pitt returns to his chair behind the desk and sets the Longhorn on the desktop.

Silence.

Billy scratches his neck. "You know, Mr. Pitt, um, your wife, she, well, she sure thought I was getting paid a lot for that hit. So does the guy on the phone. I ain't complaining, you know. I mean, you been real good to me and all, but this is really starting to get hairy. First her, now this guy. Sort of, you know, like what you might call above and beyond the call of duty, if you know what I mean? Sort of."

Pitt stares at him. "Billy, you are going to have to learn how to be patient. You have made one serious mistake in this matter. You are going to meet that mistake in person tomorrow night. And when you do, you will be carrying a briefcase filled with twenty-five thousand dollars. It's going to be just you and him. You get the information from him, then you eliminate the mistake, and then the money is yours, Billy. You will have earned it."

Billy grins. "Jeez, that's great, Mr. Pitt. Twenty-five large, huh? Damn. Don't worry about that guy, Mr. Pitt. He's as good as dead already. No more mistakes, sir. I promise."

"Fine. We will talk in the morning." Pitt gestures toward the door. "Good night."

Billy gets to his feet. "Yes, sir."

Billy puts the bullets into the front pocket of his jacket and tucks the Walther into his shoulder holster "No more mistakes. I'll earn that money, sir. I promise."

He pauses in the doorway and turns back to smile. "Good night, Mr. Pitt."

Pitt nods.

Chapter Forty

A drum roll of rain awakens Hal with a start. He'd been sleeping slumped against the passenger window. Rubbing his neck, he checks his watch: four-twenty-seven a.m. Milton is seated behind the steering wheel, staring straight ahead.

"Anything happening?" Hal asks.

Milton shakes his head.

Hal wipes his hand along the windshield and peers through. "Jeez."

The rain is coming in waves, thundering across the roof, clattering down the hood, crackling along the street. Two buildings down, under a blurred streetlamp, sits Bledsoe's black Mustang. Hal zips up his windbreaker and takes a stick of black licorice from the bag on the front seat.

He turns to Milton. "Get some sleep, Bro. I can watch for awhile."

Milton stretches against the steering wheel. "Maybe I will."

"Hey, how's Peggy doing?"

"I talked to her tonight. She's holding up. Not too thrilled."

"Man, she's a real trooper."

"I put them on the plane yesterday."

"How about the girls? They okay?"

"Peggy says they're having fun with their grandparents."

"Oh, yeah, that's right. They're all staying with her folks?"

Milton nods.

"Cleveland, right?"

"Suburb. Beachwood."

"Those girls of yours are so cute. I love 'em."

"They love their Uncle Hal, that is for sure."

The two of them listen to the rain, the windshield fogging up again.

"Guess who came to visit me on my last day in jail?"

Milton turns to his brother. "Who?"

"Moran."

"The detective?"

"Yep."

Milton snorts. "That's outrageous. A flagrant violation. He is not allowed to do that."

"No, no, no. We didn't talk about the case."

"Oh? Then what did you talk about?"

"Baseball."

"You talked about baseball?"

"Turns out he played two years of semi-pro. Figured he wasn't going any higher. Gave that up, tried life insurance for awhile. Said he couldn't stomach having to peddle that stuff to all his pals. Took the police exam on a lark, passed, and decided, 'Why not?' Still plays ball, though. He's on some police league team. Softball, though."

As Milton studies his brother, he tugs on his right earlobe.

"What?" Hal finally says.

"You think he likes you?"

Hal shrugs. "I guess so. I mean, as much as you can like someone in jail for kidnapping and murder. Why?"

Milton frowns. "He might be the one."

"What one?"

"Who we call."

"When?"

"When we have what we need."

"I'm not following you, Bro."

Milton yawns. "I shall explain that later."

He folds his jacket in half and uses it as a pillow as he rests his head against the window. "Keep an eye out."

"Will do, Bro. Get some shut-eye."

Chapter Forty-one

Milton awakes to the sound of the car door opening. It's Hal, returning with a McDonald's bag.

"Morning, Bro."

Milton rubs his eyes. "Anything happen last night?"

"All quiet." Hal opens the bag. "Rain didn't last long. Got us some coffee and Egg McMuffins.

He hands a cup to Milton. "Need sugar or cream?"

Milton shakes his head.

Hal grins. "You like it black, eh? Like your women."

Milton frowns. "Pardon?

"*Airplane*, Bro. The movie."

Hal hands him an Egg McMuffin in the wrapper and a couple napkins.

"Thank you, Hal."

"My pleasure."

They eat in silence. The sky is cloudy.

Hal asks, "Want another? Got us each two."

Milton wipes his mouth with his napkin. "I'm good for now. Thanks."

Another ten minutes pass.

"Wow," Hal says, "this feels like one of those cop movies. You know, the stakeout part."

Milton nods, staring at Bledsoe's apartment.

"You're a rightie, right?"

Milton turns toward Hal with a frown. "What do you mean?"

"Right-handed."

"I am."

"Perfect. I put two gloves in the trunk. You can have your old catcher's mitt. Finish your coffee and I'll show you my stuff."

"Really?" Milton looks at Hal and shrugs. "This morning?"

"Sure. We're just sitting here doing nothing. I bet that creep is still asleep. It'll be fun, Bro. Just like old times in our backyard, right?"

Milton sighs. "I suppose."

Back when Milton was in high school and Hal was in middle school, Milton would occasionally help Hal work on his pitches in the backyard. Milton had no interest in baseball—or any sport, for that matter. But Hal, who worshipped his big brother, saved up his allowance and bought Milton a used catcher's mitt. After their father died a year later, Milton started working with his younger brother once or twice a week. He'd catch—or at least try to catch—and Hal would pitch. Milton didn't like the crouch position, so he brought out a short stool to sit on when Hal pitched to him. Fortunately, even back then Hal had such good control that Milton rarely had to move his glove more than a few inches.

"I got a mean curve, Bro. You're not going to believe it."

Milton took a sip of his coffee. "Okay."

"By the way, you got some weird stuff in your trunk."

"I did some shopping for us on Amazon."

"What kind of flashlight did you get?"

"Not a flashlight. That piece of equipment is a stun gun."

Hal's eyes widen. "Really? Like one of those Tasers?"

"Similar."

"For what?"

"I shall explain in detail later. It all will depend upon how this scenario plays out."

"Yeah, like, what is the scenario?"

"Again, Hal, all in good time."

"Cool."

Forty minutes later, Hal wipes the sweat from his forehead and takes a breath. The breeze flutters his windbreaker.

"Okay," he says.

Hal and Milton are down the street from Bledsoe's apartment building. Hal has his back to the building. He's partially shielded by a dumpster. About sixty feet further down the street, Milton faces Hal. He has on the catcher's mitt.

With a grunt, Milton squats and puts two fingers down. Curve. Then he gives Hal the target.

Hal nods, winds, and pitches.

The pitch comes in on the left of Milton but dips down into the strike zone in the last several feet and thunks into the catcher's mitt. Milton shakes his head in wonder. He never had to move the catcher's mitt. He stands and tosses the ball back toward Hal, who catches it on a bounce.

"I'm warm," Hal says. "Let's try a heater."

"A what?"

"Fastball."

Milton nods, grunts as he squats, puts one finger down, and then gives Hal the target.

Hal grins as he goes into a full wind-up and pitches. The ball whacks into the catcher's mitt, knocking Milton back onto his butt.

Milton smiles. "Single to left."

"No way, Bro. That's strike three."

Hal throws another dozen or so pitches, each hitting the target, popping the catcher's mitt.

He takes off his glove and tosses it to Milton. "You try, Bro. I'll catch."

"I can't pitch."

"Sure you can. We'll start off closer together."

They trade gloves. Hal stands Milton about thirty feet away. He squats, bangs the catcher's mitt with his fist a few times, and says, "Let's see what you got, Mr. Gibson."

Milton winds, looking every bit the former president of the high school chess club, throws a pitch that bounces to Hal's right and bangs off the dumpster.

Hal trots back to get the ball, but when he turns around Milton is running toward him.

"What?" Hal says.

"It's Bledsoe.

They run back to Milton's car. Milton climbs in behind the wheel and starts the engine as Hal gets in the passenger side, tosses the catcher's mitt into the backseat, and shoves the baseball into the pocket of his windbreaker.

• • ● • •

Thirty minutes later, they watch as the black Mustang parks in a No Parking zone in front of an eight-story office building on Locust Avenue downtown. Milton pulls his car into a space on the other side of the street, several cars back from the Mustang.

Bledsoe gets out of his car and walks into the building.

"Is that where Pitt's office is?" Hal asks.

Milton nods.

They wait.

And wait.

And finally, Bledsoe walks out of the building carrying a briefcase.

Milton chuckles. "Well, well, well."

He starts the engine.

They follow Bledsoe's Mustang back to his house and watch as he gets out and walks back into his apartment carrying the briefcase.

"Houston," Milton announces, "Tranquility Base here. The Eagle has landed."

Hal frowns. "Huh?"

Chapter Forty-two

"The River Des Peres."

Hal frowns. "The sewer? You want to meet him in the sewer?"

"Not in the sewage part. That's underground."

"Where are you talking?"

"The section above ground. That stormwater sewer. Right where it comes out of those tunnels at Macklind."

"Tunnels? What tunnels?"

Milton sighs. "I will show you." He starts the engine. "As you will see, it is ideal for tonight's rendezvous."

Twenty minutes later, driving south on Macklind Avenue, Milton slows the car as they rumble across the railroad tracks and then pulls to a stop halfway along the overpass that runs above a large culvert.

"There," he says, pointing to his left out the driver's window.

Hal leans forward to look out Milton's window. "Whoa!"

Hal stares at the tunnel openings—two huge ones, side by side, horseshoe-shaped, each tall enough and wide enough for a semi-trailer truck to drive through. To the right of those two openings is a third one, much smaller, slightly angled away from the other two, just tall enough for a man to enter. The overpass where they sit is about fifty yards from the tunnel openings. Hal squints. Along the concrete wall above the tunnels is etched: 1928 DES PERES DRAINAGE WORKS.

All three tunnels open onto the concrete culvert. The culvert's side walls are maybe twenty feet high, each side angled outward in a wide V-shape and ending in the downward sloping embankment of earth and gravel that rises on either side above culvert.

Hal turns to look out his window in the direction away from the tunnel openings. The culvert runs beneath the overpass and continues on, passing beneath another overpass about three blocks further down, and then another one further down in a left-curving line until it disappears in the distance.

He turns back toward the tunnel openings.

A thin stream of water flows out of the center tunnel and runs down the middle of the culvert and beneath the overpass. Scattered on the cracked cement of the culvert in front of the center tunnel entrance are several tree branches, a battered and rusted shopping cart on its side, some empty plastic grocery bags, a bicycle tire, a mangled car fender, and what looks like a broken broomstick.

Hal turns back to Milton with a befuddled frown. "What is this, Bro?"

"The River Des Peres." Milton points out Hal's window down the culvert in the opposite direction of the tunnels. "It goes all the way down to the Mississippi. About nine miles from here."

"But back there," Hal says, pointing toward the tunnels. "The river runs underground?"

"Only through Forest Park."

"Why there?"

"Back when it was a real river, the River Des Peres ran through the middle of Forest Park. Wreaked havoc every spring. So almost a century ago they dug a huge trench two miles long right through Forest Park and built the two big tunnels and this culvert. It was one of the largest engineering projects in the country back then."

"Why two tunnels?"

"One carries the stormwater and the other carries the sewage. The sewage portion drops even further underground before it reaches the end of that tunnel. It runs beneath this culvert to a treatment plant near the Mississippi River. The one you see, the one with the water coming out, that's the one that empties into the river. The other one serves as the backup during big rains."

Hal peers down at the culvert and shakes his head. "Not much water down there."

"Not now, but you should see it after a major rainstorm. All the stormwater sewers from the north side empty into the River Des Peres, and by the time that water comes pouring out of those two tunnels it's up to the top of that culvert, sometimes near the top of the embankment."

"Wow."

"It can be dangerous. People have drowned."

"How do you know all this, Bro?"

Milton smiles. "My firm represents the Metropolitan Sewer District. MSD. I worked on a lawsuit for them during my first years at the firm. MSD was sued by the Missouri Department of Natural Resources. Nasty case. A big part involved some environmental issues with the tunnels. I spent a lot of time down in those tunnels—sometimes a full day—with our expert witnesses. That's how I knew."

"Knew what?"

"That this is the perfect spot to meet Bledsoe."

"Here? On this overpass?"

Milton laughs. "Up here? No way."

"Then where?"

"Down there. Right at the entrance to that middle tunnel."

Hal turns toward the tunnels, stares at the opening, and then turns back to his big brother with a frown. "Huh?"

"The perfect spot. The acoustics are excellent."

"Acoustics? What does that matter? We're not taping a concert."

"I'm hoping we're taping a confession."

"What do you mean?"

"Actually, you will be doing the taping. I shall be near the mouth of the tunnel and you shall be safely inside. Far enough back to be invisible but close enough to tape it."

"Bro, I'm like totally lost here."

"I will explain everything, Hal. I have been working on this since last night. I have it all mapped out."

Chapter Forty-three

"I've been thinking, Bro. I don't know about this plan of yours."

"What's the problem?"

"Mr. Pitt. I can't believe he wants Bledsoe to just give you the money tonight. I bet he wants him to kill you."

"Perhaps." Milton shrugs. "But not until Bledsoe finds out whether I have an accomplice. That is what should be of most concern to him. He needs to know the answer to that, and if I do have an accomplice, he needs to know that person's name."

"Here you go, boys."

They look up at the waitress, a woman in her sixties with bright red lipstick and dyed black hair in a bun. She has two plates, each with a hamburger and fries.

"Medium rare for you, honey," she says to Hal as she sets down his plate.

She turns to Milton with a big smile. "And medium well for you, darling."

They are seated in a booth near the back of O'Connell's Pub. It's nearly one-thirty, and the lunch crowd has largely dispersed.

"Another beer, boys?" she asks.

Milton shakes his head. "I'm good."

Hal nods. "Me, too."

Hal puts some ketchup on his burger and some more on his plate for the fries. He hands the bottle to Milton and frowns.

"What?" Milton says.

"So he wants to know if you have an accomplice? What are you going to tell him?"

"I'll string him along, get him talking."

"But what about the case against Pitt?"

"That's your job."

"My job? What do you mean?"

"You're going to have my cell phone. It can record a conversation, just like a Dictaphone. I'll get him talking, and you'll get it all on tape. Once he fingers Pitt, we've got him dead to rights."

"You really think he will?"

"I hope so. But even if he doesn't, we'll get enough on tape for an arrest. As long as he shows up with money, I'll get him to say something incriminating. The police can work him after they arrest him, maybe get a confession."

"The police? How are they involved?"

Milton grins. "That's going to be part of your job tonight."

"My job? Good grief, Milton."

"Well, boys?"

The look up. It's their waitress smiling down at them. "How is everything?"

Hal forces a smile. "Delicious."

She nods her head. "Glad to hear."

After she leaves, Hal says, "How do we even get down there?"

"To the tunnels? Easy. The railroad tracks run along the top of the culvert on the north side. You could climb down from there, but it's easier on the other side. There is a gravel path on that side. There is a chain across the path at Macklind and a sign that says it's for MSD employees only. But it is, I emphasize, just a chain. You can duck under it or skirt around it and then walk down the path until you are even with the tunnel openings. There is a stairway right there. It takes you down to the culvert."

"And that's where we'll be?"

"We will be waiting for him inside the tunnel when he arrives. We'll have placed a folding chair right at the entrance. Facing out. That is where I tell him to sit. To simply sit and wait."

"And then?"

Milton grins. "And then it is show time."

"Show time?"

Milton nods and takes a bit of his hamburger.

Hal shakes his head. "I don't know. This ain't exactly Hollywood. We're talking a sewer line in south St. Louis."

Chapter Forty-four

Later that afternoon, Milton is standing on his backyard patio, the cell phone pressed against his ear.

Peggy answers. "Hi."

Her voice is subdued.

"Hi, honey," Milton says, trying to sound upbeat and casual. "So how are you doing?"

"We're fine, Milton. Fine. Now what's going on there?"

"Not much. We are just in the process of wrapping things up here. I am thinking that you and the girls might be able to come home the day after tomorrow."

"What does that mean?"

"As I said, we are just in the process of wrapping things up."

Peggy sighs. "Milton."

"What, honey?"

"I'm going crazy. I can't sleep. I am so worried."

"Don't worry, Peggy. We will be fine. I promise. It will all be over tomorrow."

"What will all be over?"

"This whole mess I got Hal into."

"Milton, you didn't get Hal into this mess. Dammit, Milton. You're blind. Your idiot brother got himself into that mess. All on his very own."

Hal is standing off to the side on the grass. He watches his older brother on the phone as he tosses the baseball in the air underhanded, catching it in his glove, tossing it up again, catching it.

Milton glances over at Hal and takes a few steps toward the far side of the patio. "We'll be fine," he whispers. And then, "Can I talk to the girls?"

"They're with my mom. She took them shopping."

"Oh. Well, maybe I can talk to them later."

"I didn't mean to yell at you, Milton."

"That's okay, honey."

"I'm sorry."

"No need to apologize."

"It's just I'm so worried for you. You're not Dirty Harry, Milton, and you're not Rambo."

"I am fully cognizant of those facts."

"This isn't a movie, honey. Just be careful."

"That is my middle name."

"Oh?" Peggy laughs. "I thought it was Isadore." A pause, and then, "I love you, Milton."

"I love you, Peggy."

Silence.

Milton finally says, "Goodbye, lover."

"Goodbye, honey. Be careful."

Milton puts the cell phone back in his pants pocket and turns toward his brother.

"Everything good?" Hal asks.

Milton smiles and nods. "Couldn't be better."

"She's worried, isn't she?"

"A little."

"I don't blame her. I'm worried, too."

"No need to. The plan is working. Bledsoe has the money. He's waiting for the call, and we shall be waiting for him at the drop point. I will all be over tonight, Hal."

"I hope so."

Milton grinned. "I know so."

Hal sighed. "Oh, boy. I'm nervous. Hey, want to play some catch?"

"Again?"

"Come on, Bro. Maybe it'll calm me down. We can do a pretend game."

"What's that?"

"I'll pitch, you catch. Balls and strikes. You can call them. It'll be fun."

"Really?" Milton rolls his eyes. "Okay."

"Awesome. I'll get your catcher's mitt."

Chapter Forty-five

Hal hands Milton the folding chair. He watches Milton set it even with the mouth of the middle tunnel, facing out into the culvert.

Milton steps back, looks at the chair admiringly, and nods. "That should do it."

"You're going to have him sit there?"

"I am, indeed. Until I come out of the tunnel. We'll switch then."

"It's going to be nighttime, Milton. How are you going see what's going on?"

Milton pointed up. "See that spotlight above the tunnels? It goes on at night. We'll have plenty of light."

A gust of wind rattles the folding chair. The temperature has been dropping. It's now around forty-five degrees. The forecast has it dropping to into the upper thirties that evening.

Hal zips up his windbreaker and takes a few steps into the tunnel. "So I'm, like, in here?"

"We both are until he arrives. You will stay back to record our conversation, and then you will call the police."

Hal looks up, scanning the arched ceiling. "When do I make that call?"

"As soon I get him to say something incriminating. I will give you a signal."

"With your hand?"

Milton thinks it over. "No. Too risky. We'll use a code word."

"What's the code word?"

Milton looks around as he ponders the question. He smiles. "Sewage."

"Sewage?"

"Fits the location nicely. As soon as I say it, you'll dial 9-1-1."

"Not Detective Moran?"

"No. He's out in the county. Too far away. We can't wait that long. We'll need St. Louis cops. We can call Moran once the local cops arrive."

Hal takes out his cell phone. "How far back am I going to be?"

Milton studies the chair and then the tunnel and then the chair again. "About twenty yards."

Hal walks further into the tunnel and turns. "About here?"

Milton nods. "That's good."

Hal stares down at his cell phone. "Uh, we got a problem."

"What?"

"Got no reception in here."

Milton grimaces. "Shit."

"Oh, Jeez, Milton, are we screwed? What are we going to do?"

"No big deal. We'll use my phone."

"I don't think you'll get reception either."

"I'll have the phone with me out front. I'll have reception out there. You'll use my Bluetooth device. It's good up to ninety feet."

"I don't understand."

"I'll punch in 9-1-1 before he arrives. Then I'll set the phone to record the conversation. It'll be clearer out here anyway. You'll be able to hear it on the Bluetooth, too. When it's time, I'll say the code word and you can press the Dial button on the device. The only place the phone will ring is in your earbud. When the police answer, you'll cover your mouth and quietly tell them where we are and that it's an emergency."

"They'll know how to get here?"

"Oh, definitely. Crazy stuff goes on down here all the time. Mostly drug deals. I found that out when I worked on that matter for the Sewer District. Cops are down here at least one a month."

Hal looks around the tunnel and shakes his head. "Man, this place is unreal."

"It certainly is unique." Milton smiles. "And if everything goes off as planned, you'll be a free man by tomorrow."

"Boy, I sure hope it works."

Hal walks back out of the tunnel to where Milton is standing by the chair. He gestures toward the gym bag at Milton's feet. "So where'd you get all that stuff?"

"Online."

"Really? You can buy a bulletproof vest online?"

Milton nods. "Amazon sells them."

"And that mask?"

"Amazon."

"Wow. And it's bulletproof, too?"

"Army grade. The same brand the police SWAT teams use."

Hal smiles. "Awesome. He's going freak out when he sees you. Especially with that mask. Like he's stepped into a remake of that Halloween movie."

Milton nods. "That certainly is one of the strategies. Throw him off balance."

Hal looks around—the culvert, the tunnels, the overpass in the distance.

Another gust of wind.

He turns to his older brother. "So what's next?"

"I call him. Set up the meeting."

"When do you do that?"

Milton checks his watch. "We want him to get here when it's dark. It'll be dark by seven. We don't want to give him too much advance warning. His apartment is maybe fifteen minutes from here. I'll call him around six-thirty."

Clang!

Clang!

Clang!

"What's that?" Hal says.

The clanging continues.

"Freight train." Milton points toward the overpass. "See those flashing red lights?"

Clang!

Clang!

Hal squints. He sees the flashing lights and the railroad crossing bars lowering on either side of the railroad tracks on the northern edge of the overpass.

The clanging continues.

Approaching from the west is a yellow locomotive with a Union Pacific logo along its side. Actually two locomotives, moving maybe fifteen miles an hour. They are pulling a line of flat cars and box cars that stretches behind out of sight. A pickup truck waits behind the crossing bar on the south side of the tracks, smoky vapors curling out of its exhaust pipe.

The lead locomotive blasts its horn as it passes the overpass above the north side of the culvert. The two locomotives rumble past Hal and Milton, who watch from below.

The clanging continues, now joined by the squeaking and grinding of flat cars and the box cars. The queue of idling automobiles on the south side of the tracks—the side barely visible from where they are standing—is starting to grow. Now three. Then a fourth. And then a brown UPS truck.

"How often do these trains come?" Hal asks.

"Several times a day."

"I hope we don't get one tonight."

"Shouldn't be a problem."

"What if the engineer looks down here?"

Milton smiles. "He will just see two guys talking."

"Let's hope that's all he sees."

Chapter Forty-six

Bledsoe turns off the TV, lights another Tiparillo, stands, checks his watch, shakes his head, and walks into the kitchen. He opens the refrigerator, takes out a can of Busch, pops the tab, takes a big sip, closes the refrigerator, walks over to the sink, and stares out the window. It's starting to get dark.

The telephone rings. He waits until the third ring and lifts the receiver.

"Yeah?"

"Got the money?"

"I got it."

"Then listen careful, Billy. This is going to happen thirty minutes from now. You're not there by seven and I go to the cops. Understand?"

Bledsoe checks his wristwatch. six-twenty-seven p.m.

"Yeah."

"You got a pencil and paper?"

"Uh, just a second." A pause. "Okay."

"Listen careful. Get onto Macklind from Oakland. Just south of Manchester you'll pass over some rail-road tracks and then an overpass. Look east down that culvert. You'll see three tunnel openings—two big ones and one small one to the right. Park your car. Walk down that gravel path toward those tunnels. You will come to a stairway. Go down it. When you get to the bottom, you will see a chair right in front of the middle tunnel. That is where you will sit. Understand?"

Bledsoe is scribbling notes. "In front of the middle tunnel. Yeah."

What's the money in?"

"A briefcase."

"Good. Sit your butt in that chair. Put the briefcase on the ground on your left side. Make sure you are in that chair by seven sharp. That's where I will meet you. Got it?"

"A gravel path?"

"You can't miss it. There is a waist-high chain across the path. Just walk around it."

"Okay."

"Seven, Billy. Don't be late and you won't be sorry."

There's a click, and then a dial tone.

Bledsoe stares at the receiver and then hangs up.

"Fuck you, you fucking fuck. Fuck you."

He looks at the directions he scribbled on the note-pad, reads through them. He checks his watch, lifts the receiver, and dials a number.

Pitt answers. "Well?"

"He just called, Mr. Pitt."

"When and where?"

"Seven."

"Tonight?"

"Yes, sir."

"Where?"

"It's kind of weird."

"Where, Billy?"

"Okay. You got a pencil and paper?"

Stage 5:
The Release

Chapter Forty-seven

The folding chair is right where that asshole said it would be: sitting in front of the big middle tunnel opening. Bledsoe spots it when he's halfway along the gravel path that runs parallel above the culvert. A dim spotlight atop the tunnel illuminates the chair in a dull, yellowish light. Bledsoe stops, looks around, and then leans over to peer down the gravel embankment to the culvert.

No one else in sight. He reaches inside his jacket again to touch the shoulder holster.

Bastard's probably waiting inside one of the fucking tunnels.

Bledsoe continues down the path, the briefcase in his right hand. The path ends above the tunnels. A concrete stairway leads down to the culvert. A waist-high chain, connected on either side to a metal pole, hangs across the top of the stairway. He steps around the chain and starts down, moving carefully, the stairs faintly lit by the moon above.

He reaches the bottom and steps onto the culvert in front of the tunnels. No movement. No sound above the trickle of the water coming out of the middle tunnel, the thin stream passing through the legs of the folding chair.

He checks his watch.

7:03.

He takes a deep breath and slowly exhales.

Okay, man. It's show time.

Bledsoe walks over to the chair and looks around again. Nothing visible inside the tunnel. He takes a seat, his back to the tunnel, and sets the briefcase down on the left side.

And waits.

A minute.

Two minutes.

And then, "Good evening, Billy."

He flinches.

Same voice from those phone calls. Somewhere from behind him—inside the tunnel, but not far away.

"Before we discuss this transaction, Billy, you will need to remove your jacket."

Shit.

Bledsoe turns his head to the right but he can't see the speaker.

"I said remove your jacket."

"But it's chilly."

"I am holding a Taser gun aimed at you, sir. I'd prefer not to use it, but I will do so if you don't remove your coat. And do so slowly."

Bledsoe thinks it over, weighs his options, and unzips his jacket.

"Take it off and drop it on the ground to your right.

Bledsoe follows directions.

"My, my, my. Raise your arms."

Bledsoe raises his arms.

The speaker reaches around and removes the gun from the shoulder holster.

"You came here armed? I'm disappointed in you, Billy."

"I always carry that, man. No offense. It's dark out there. Shit, I brought you the fucking money. The gun's no big deal."

"That's for me to decide. Now stand up and turn around. Slowly."

Bledsoe follows directions.

He stares, eyes wide, trying to make sense of what he sees. The speaker is shorter than him. He's wearing a bulky windbreaker and what looks like a goddamn Halloween mask—black with eye holes and a steel mesh mouth opening. In his right hand the man is pointing at him what looks like a fucking flashlight on steroids. He's holding Bledsoe's handgun in his left hand.

"One last thing," the masked man says. "Drop your pants."

"My pants?"

"You heard me. Drop your pants and then we can do our business and you can leave."

"My pants? What the fuck, man?"

"You got five seconds, Billy. Five. Four. Three. Two. One. Zero. Blastoff."

A bolt of lightning shoots out of the flashlight and strikes Bledsoe in the chest.

"Yeow!"

Bledsoe drops to the ground, thrashing in pain

The man stands over him, pointing the flashlight at his stomach. "Don't make me do this again." And now he points the gun. "Or this. Stand up and drop your pants."

Wincing, Bledsoe staggers to his feet. "Man, this is fucked."

"Drop your pants, Billy."

Bledsoe loosens his belt, unzips his trousers, and lowers them to the ground.

"What is that down there?"

Bledsoe looks down. Below his boxer shorts, strapped to his left calf is a hunting knife. He looks up with a shit-eating grin, his face glistening with sweat.

"Planning on a little hunting tonight, Billy? We seem to have some genuine trust issues here. Take it off. Slowly. That's it. Now toss it over there. All the way over."

The knife clanks against the cement.

"There you go. Good. Now take three steps back from the chair."

Bledsoe steps back, his pants gathered at his ankles.

The man comes forward, steps around the chair, and sits down on the chair facing Bledsoe, the Taser weapon pointed at Bledsoe's crotch.

"What are you going to do?" Bledsoe asks.

"I haven't decided."

"Oh, man. Don't fuck with me. I brought you the money. It's right there."

"You also brought a gun and knife."

"And the money. That's what you asked me to do. That's major."

"Let us start all over. From the top. You are Billy Bledsoe, correct?"

"Yeah."

"You brought me some money, correct?"

"Yeah."

"To be precise, you brought twenty-five thousand dollars in cash, correct?"

"Yeah."

"And that money is in the briefcase you brought here, correct?"

"That's what I said."

"And that money is part of our discussion, correct?"

"Yeah."

"And what is our discussion, Billy?"

"I give you the money and you don't tell no one."

"I don't tell no one what?"

"About the motel. About Cherry."

"You mean about you killing Cherry?"

"Whatever."

"No, say it, Billy. That was our conversation. You give me the money and I won't tell anyone what?"

"About Cherry. About, you know, about me and about her dying and, well, you know."

"About you killing her, right?"

Bledsoe frowns. He stands there with his pants bunched down at his ankles, his boxer shorts fluttering in the chilly wind.

"Billy?"

"What?"

"Let's make sure we are clear about our deal. You don't want me to tell anyone what?"

"About me and Cherry, about killing her."

"About you killing her, correct?"

Bledsoe takes a deep breath and nods."

"Out loud, Billy. Say it."

"About me killing her."

"There. That wasn't so hard."

"Jeez, man, I'm freezing here. It's cold."

"We're almost done, Billy."

"Come on, man. Hurry up."

"It wasn't your idea, was it?"

Bledsoe frowns. "What wasn't?"

"Killing her."

"Hey, this is bullshit. I brought the fucking money. That was the fucking deal."

"And you also brought the fucking gun and the fucking knife, and that wasn't the fucking deal."

"I don't get it. What do you want?"

"Maybe more money."

"Oh, come on, man."

Now the man raises the gun. "We both know this isn't your money. Who gave you this money?"

"Huh?"

"You heard me. Who gave you this money?"

"You want more money, I can get more. Give me a couple days. I'll get more."

"From who?"

Clang!

Clang!

Clang!

Bledsoe turns toward the sound. In the distance the red railroad crossing lights are flashing.

Bledsoe turns back, eyes wide. "What the hell?"

"Just a train coming, Billy. Back to business here. You said you could get more money. From who?"

Hal edges a few steps closer, adjusting the earpiece with left hand, resting his finger lightly on the Dial button.

Bledsoe is maybe sixty feet away, facing Milton, facing Hal. The briefcase is upright on the left side of the chair.

Over the clanging comes the rumble of a train. This one is moving much faster than the freight train.

Come on, Hal whispers, his heart racing. *We got what we need. Say the code word.*

In a louder voice Milton says, "From who, Billy?"

"He'll pay more. I know he will. But first I gotta be able to tell him you're in this alone."

"What does that mean?"

It's getting harder to hear them as the train approaches.

"Are you the only one, man?" Bledsoe shouts. "Anyone else in on this?"

"None of your business, Billy. Your only business is getting me the money. And the only question you have to answer is from who. I know you don't have that kind of money. So answer that question and you can leave safe and sound. Who?"

Come on, Bro. Sewage. Say the word.

The Amtrak locomotive whistle blows as the cars rush by.

"Who?" Milton shouts.

"My boss."

"Leonard Pitt?"

Bledsoe nods.

"Is that a yes?"

"Yes."

"Did he have you kill his wife?"

Bledsoe says something, but Hal can't hear it.

"What?" Milton shouts.

There's a CRACK of gunshot, muffled by the train noise.

Hal watches in horror as Milton lurches sideways off the chair to the right, the gun and the Taser skittering across the concrete as he grabs his thigh, the blood already seeping between his fingers.

Chapter Forty-eight

The train noises fade in the distance as Bledsoe yanks up his pants and fastens his belt.

Milton is on his side, writhing in pain, his hand clutching his bloody thigh. The cell phone has dropped out of Milton's jacket. It rests on the concrete just beyond his head. He reaches for it and pulls it toward him.

Just as Hal starts forward, Bledsoe turns toward the stairway.

"Who's there?" Bledsoe calls.

Hal freezes.

Out of the darkness steps Leonard Pitt. He's wearing a dark raincoat. In his gloved right hand he has a long-barreled revolver.

"Jeez," says Bledsoe, "nice shooting, Mr. Pitt. You sure nailed that bastard."

Pitt doesn't respond, doesn't even acknowledge Bledsoe. Hal tenses as Pitt pauses to lean over Milton's body. Pitt straightens and walks over to where the handgun lies on the cement. He puts the long-barreled revolver in his left hand, bends down, picks up the handgun with his right hand, and straightens as he turns back to face Bledsoe.

"Wow," Bledsoe says as Pitt approaches. "I about shit my pants when I heard that shot, Mr. Pitt."

Pitt is surveying the area.

Bledsoe glances at the gun in Pitt's left hand.

"Hey, I didn't know you owned a Longhorn, too."

"I don't." Pitt hands the gun to Bledsoe. "It's yours."

"Yeah, it looked kind of familiar. But...but aren't you worried they might trace it back to me?"

"I am not worried, Billy. I assume they will trace the Longhorn back to you and trace this Smith & Wesson"—he pauses and gestures toward Milton with the handgun—"back to this creep."

Bledsoe frowns. "I don't get it."

"You never did, Billy."

Pitt points the handgun at Bledsoe's chest and fires. Bledsoe staggers backward, his mouth moving, no words coming out. Pitt shoots him again as Bledsoe stumbles back onto the slanted wall of the culvert, the Longhorn clattering to the ground. He looks up at Pitt with a baffled frown as he slides down into a sitting position. His frown fades, his eyes roll upward, and his head lowers onto his chest. Pitt watches the body list to the side and fall, Bledsoe's head conking onto the cement.

Pitt turns back to Milton.

Hal knows Milton's time is running out. This is it. He's got to save him.

And that's when he realizes he's squeezing the baseball. He removes it from his windbreaker pocket just as Pitt reaches Milton.

Pitt is standing sideways to Hal. Maybe sixty feet away, like a right-handed batter.

Shit! Maybe.

Pitt leans over Milton.

"Can you hear me, asshole?" Pitt says.

Still leaning over, the gun still in his right hand, Pitt says again, "You hear me?"

Hal goes into his wind-up, all muscle-memory now. As he pivots and leans back, his left leg rising, he shouts, Hey!!'"

Pitt straightens in surprise, raising the handgun, still standing sideways to Hal.

Pitt squints into the darkness of the tunnel and fires the gun just as Hal releases the ball.

Like so many key moments in Hal's aborted career, what happens next seems to unfold in slow motion.

—the bullet zinging past Hal's left ear—

—the ball spinning toward Pitt—

—Pitt's eyes widening as out of the darkness he spots the oncoming ball—

—Hal finishing the follow-through—

—Pitt's head pulling back—

—the baseball smacking against Pitt's left temple—

—Pitt's legs crumpling—

—the gun discharging toward the sky—

—Pitt toppling backwards, his head banging against concrete—

Silence.

And then, "Milton!"

Hal sprints toward his big brother.

Stage 6:
The Follow-Through

Chapter Forty-nine

Milton didn't find out until the day he was released.

That was Day 3.

Hal had spent that first night in Milton's hospital room, sleeping on a cot the orderly had brought in.

"You're good, Bro," Hal told him when Milton awoke on Day 1. "They got the bullet out, sewed you up. No bone damage. Should be going home in a couple days. Surgeon said he'll be in around noon to check on you. Pakistani, I think. Or maybe Indian. Can never tell the difference. Dr. Khan. Like Genghis. Good dude."

"What about Peggy?"

"Called her an hour ago. She's flying back today. With the girls. All is good.

"So what exactly happened?"

"They arrested Pitt. He shot Bledsoe. Killed him."

"What happened to Pitt?"

Hal chuckled. "He's two floors up. Cops guarding his room."

"But what happened that night?"

Hal grins. "Good thing you warmed me up. Nailed him with a fastball high and tight. My first beanball. Knocked him out cold. Asshole was still out when the cops arrived. Gave the cops your cell phone. You got everything on tape, even the shooting. Cops took my statement down at the station last night. Didn't let me go 'til two in the morning. But all is good. Pitt is in some deep shit. Two Murder Ones, according to Moran, plus a bunch of other nasty charges."

On Day 2, Milton gave his statement. Moran was there, along with two other homicide detectives and prosecutors from the City and the County.

After the others left the room, Moran leaned over Milton's bed, grinned, and shook his head. "You are one crazy motherfucker, Bernstein. Don't know whether you deserve a Purple Heart or a rubber room in the psycho ward, but you got it done, pal. I'll give you that much. You nailed that prick to the cross. Even if he lives to a hundred, he's gonna die behind bars."

He gave Milton a fist bump before he left.

Also on Day 2, the physical therapist had him up and walking. The first time with a walker, down the hall and back. The second time unassisted.

But he didn't watch any TV in the hospital. Never been a TV guy, especially with the cable news stations. Couldn't stomach them.

Instead, Milton spent most of Day 2 doing what he loved the most: working on court papers. Specifically, drafting a motion to compel in *In re Bottles & Cans*, the massive antitrust case that his law firm—and dozens of other firms around the nation—had been involved in for more than three decades. He'd called the office from his hospital bed on the afternoon of Day 1, explained the new developments including the anticipated dismissal of all charges against Hal, and arranged for the firm to deliver his laptop to the hospital. On Day 2 alone, he billed 14.3 hours working on those motion papers.

And thus he didn't find out until Day 3.

They were all there that morning—Peggy, the girls, Hal. Though he could walk by then—or, more accurately, he could limp—he had to leave in a wheelchair. Hospital rules.

Peggy went ahead with the girls to get the car. Hal pushed the wheelchair.

And that's when he found out. Or, more accurately, started to find out.

The craziness erupted the moment they passed through the sliding exit doors.

Awaiting them was a throng of reporters and photographers and videographers.

Milton looked around, stunned.

Was that Anderson Cooper over there? Geraldo Rivera?

Cameras clicking, reporters shouting, microphones pointing at him, at Hal.

"Mr. Bernstein! Over here, sir!"

"Milton! Hey, Milton! How's it feel? How's it feel to have a brother like that?"

"Over here, Milton! Were you scared?"

"Hey, Hal! You have an agent yet? Talking to any ball clubs?"

"Hal, Hal! Any movie deals?"

Peggy inches the car through the media mob, tapping on the horn as she drives forward, the hospital security guard clearing the path.

"Stand back! Let our patient through! Stand back!"

The guard helps Milton into the front seat. Hal hops in back with the girls. The cameras flash in the car windows, the reporters lean over the windshield and knock on windows even as Peggy pulls forward, a few of them jogging alongside the car, shouting unintelligible questions.

For a few moments after leaving the hospital grounds, they drive in silence.

"Good grief," Milton finally says. "Is this a slow news day?"

Peggy looks over at him "I wish. Wait 'til we get home."

"What do you mean?"

"You'll see. They've been camped out on our front lawn. CNN. Fox News. MSNBC. All the local news channels, TV vans up and down the block."

"Uncle Hal is famous, Daddy," Sara says.

"Uncle Hal?" Milton turns toward his younger brother in the backseat. "Really?"

Hal shrugs. "It's been a weird couple days, Bro."

"How so?"

Peggy sighs. "Wait until we get home, honey. I saved the papers for you."

Fortunately, they have an attached garage, which allows them to bypass the reporters and television crews on the front lawn and enter the house directly from the garage.

Milton limps over to the breakfast room table, sits down, and kisses and hugs his two daughters.

Peggy comes back into the room with an armful of newspapers—the *Post-Dispatch*, the *New York Times*, *USA Today.*

"Here you go."

She dumps the stack onto the table.

"Enjoy."

At the top of the pile is the front page section of the *Post-Dispatch* from the day after the confrontation at the tunnels. The banner headline reads:

```
COURAGEOUS EX-PITCHER
SAVES BROTHER'S LIFE;
 FELLS CORRUPT LAWYER
  WITH EPIC BEANBALL;
RECEIVES HERO'S WELCOME;
ALL CHARGES TO BE DISMISSED
```

The article—and the headlines and articles in the other papers—all tell the same story: an innocent young man, wrongfully accused of the brutal murder of the wife of a corrupt powerhouse attorney, enlists his lawyer brother to represent him. They soon find themselves in a deathtrap sprung by the corrupt attorney. Just as that corrupt attorney is about to kill the older brother, our hero, a former All-American college baseball pitcher whose promising career was cut short by a tragic motorcycle injury, somehow summons the moxie and the grit and the muscle memory to hurl a ninety-mile-per-hour fastball smack into the head of the attorney, knocking him unconscious and saving his brother's life.

The *USA Today* version got Milton's name wrong, referring to him as Marvin.

The Associated Press photographer apparently got to the scene just as the police were arriving. Standing above the culvert on the railroad track side as the police scrambled down, he took those first photographs. In the most widely disseminated shot—appearing in perhaps a dozen newspapers and hundreds of online sites and then shared on tens of thousands of Facebook pages and Twitter tweets—Hal is looking up toward the camera as he kneels beside Milton, who grimaces in pain, holding his thigh. Hal's face is a template of concern and compassion. To Hal's left, spread-eagled on his back, is Leonard Pitt, eyes closed. Behind Hal is the slumped corpse of Billy Bledsoe.

The *Buzzfeed* website Photoshopped a *Star Wars* light saber into Hal's hand and a Darth Vader mask on Pitt, with the headline: "The Force was with him!"

As Milton leafs through the newspapers, the doorbell rings.

"I'll get it," Peggy says.

"Where's Hal?"

She pauses at the doorway and gestures toward the kitchen window. "In the backyard. Playing with the girls."

She returns a few minutes later cradling a large gift-wrapped fruit-and-cheese basket and a bottle of champagne wrapped in red and white cellophane. Each has a small gift envelope attached.

"What are those?" Milton asks.

"From your law firm." Peggy sets them down on the kitchen table.

"For me?"

"The basket is. The champagne is for your brother."

She opens the back door. "Hal! Something arrived for you."

Milton opens the envelope attached to the fruit-and-cheese basket. The note reads:

> Get well soon, Milton. We're glad you're
> safe!

Best wishes for a speedy recovery,

Your colleagues at Abbott & Windsor

"Nice!" Hal says, peering over Milton's shoulder.
Milton nods. "Open yours."

Hal removes the envelope attached to the champagne bottle, takes out the note, reads it, and shakes his head.

"Jeez," his says, his face reddening, "this is getting ridiculous. Enough is enough already."

Milton reaches for the note. "Let me see."

Hal sighs and hands it to him:

A heartfelt toast to a genuine hero

We are forever grateful to you for saving Milton.

Your admirers at Abbott & Windsor

Chapter Fifty

Norman Feigelberg knocks on the door to Judge Stubbs' chambers.

No answer.

He opens the door slightly and peers in. Rahsen Ahmed stands by the picture window that looks out over the Arch and the Mississippi River. Off in the distance, a tugboat pushes a string of four barges upriver toward the Eads Bridge, the boat's propellers churning a cappuccino froth in their wake.

Rahsan turns and raises his eyebrows. "Yes, Norman?"

Norman blinks. "Oh, sorry. I was looking for the judge. I had a question about the jury instructions in the Sullivan case."

Rahsan nods toward the private bathroom.

Norman frowns. "Again?"

"Three times a charm, Norman. Come with the territory. If a man eat o' passel fiber, a man gonna evacuate a passel o' fiber."

"Is he feeling okay?"

Rahsan smiles. "Oh, he feeling much better than okay."

"Really? Why?"

"Why you think, Norman? You see today's *Post-Dispatch?*"

"Uh, no."

"Then go downstairs, buy yourself a copy, and read yourself that lead story."

Which is exactly what the Honorable Roy L. Stubbs is doing at that moment while seated on the toilet, his pants bunched around his ankles. The lead story describes the prosecutorial equivalent of a trifecta: in a joint press conference, the U.S. Attorney, the prosecutor for the City of St. Louis, and the prosecutor for St. Louis County announced the simultaneous filing of separate criminal charges against Leonard Pitt in each of those jurisdictions, including first-degree murder charges in the city (over Bledsoe's death) and the county (over Cherry Pitt's death), and various other felonies in federal court.

Judge Stubbs pauses to reread the fifth paragraph:

> When asked during the press conference, City Prosecutor Harriet Carson confirmed that she would be seeking the maximum penalty for the felony charge. "If ever a crime merited capital punishment, this one does for sure. As far as I am concerned, Leonard Pitt is the poster child for the death penalty, and I believe the jury will agree.

Judge Stubbs is grinning. "Welcome to the big leagues, Leonard."

Chapter Fifty-one

It's evening now. Dishes washed, girls in bed, and Milton seated in the den, laptop on his lap, drafting the memorandum supporting that motion to compel. He's working from home now but heads back to the office downtown Monday morning.

Peggy gazes at him from the kitchen doorway. "It drives me crazy."

Milton looks up. "What?"

"You're the one who's the hero."

He shrugs. "It's not worth fretting over."

"It is for me, Milton. You're the one who figured out who the real killer was. Not Hal. You're the one who had to deal with all those cops and prosecutors who were so convinced it was Hal that they stopped looking for the real killer. You're the one who got him out on bail. You're the one who set up that crazy rendezvous at those tunnels. Not Hal. And that, by the way, was *truly* crazy, Milton. Truly. And then you're the one who sat out there all alone that night, exposed to harm from those horrible men. Not Hal. And finally, you're the one who got shot by Pitt while Hal was standing back in the shadows inside that tunnel."

"But don't forget, Peggy—Hal saved my life. There's no denying that."

"But still. It drives me crazy." She sighs. "I'm going to get some hot tea. You want some?"

"No, thanks."

After Peggy goes into the kitchen, there's the sound of the toilet flushing. A moment later, the bathroom door opens and Hal comes into the den.

"Wow, Bro, it's good to be free again."

Milton looks up. "Agreed."

"I mean it, Milton. Without you, I'd be in jail facing life in prison."

"And without you, Hal, I'd be dead."

"Jeez, I'm getting too much credit for that. It's really embarrassing."

"But it got you that job offer, right?"

"True that! I'm psyched."

"I checked them out. The company has a good reputation."

"The people are great, their sports equipment is quality all the way, and my accounts are going to be high school coaches. Love those dudes."

"What about your baseball career?" Milton asked.

Hal grinned. "The general manager tells me they'll hold a spot in Spring training. I'll keep throwing this winter. You never know, Bro. If I can hit that creep above the ear from sixty feet out, I ought to be able to hit the corners of the plate."

"When do you start the new job?"

"In two weeks. Gave my notice at the country club yesterday. My last day is next Friday."

"They're going to miss you."

"I'll miss them, too. They've been totally nice about it. So have the members. All those moms—Jeez, they keep asking to take selfies with me."

Milton wags a finger. "No more older women, Hal."

Peggy steps into den. "How about no women, period?"

Hal laughs.

"Give that thing of yours a rest," she says.

The doorbell rings.

As Peggy starts for the door Hal holds up his hand. "That's probably for me."

He opens the door and smiles. "Hey, Patty, how's it going?"

In steps Patty, the cute lifeguard from the country club, eyes wide. "Wow," she says, gesturing over her shoulder, "it's like a total circus out there. All those reporters and cameras. It's like totally unreal."

She turns toward the den, smiles, and gives a little finger wave. "Oh, hi."

"This is Patty," Hal says.

Patty follows Hal into the den.

"You must be Mr. Bernstein," she says. "Hal's older brother."

Milton nods. "I am, indeed. And this is my wife, Peggy."

Patty smiles at Peggy. "Hi, Mrs. Bernstein. It's nice to meet you."

"Same here," Peggy says.

Patty turns back to Milton and shakes her head. "Good grief, sir. That must have been like totally scary."

Milton smiles. "I was a little nervous."

"Oh, but your brother"—she turns, gives Hal an adoring smile, and looks back at Milton—"he was like

SO awesome. We're all, like, so totally proud. I hear people at the Club keep asking for his autograph."

Hal stepped forward, embarrassed. "So we're going across the river to this club in Belleville. To hear this band. Her older brother is lead singer. Patty drove in from Mizzou for the show. I told her I'd pick her up at her house, but she wanted to meet you guys."

Patty nods. "For sure." She turns to Peggy. "It must be like so awesome to have Hal as your brother-in-law, eh?"

Peggy nods. "Sometimes it makes me tingle just to think about it."

Patty laughs. "LOL." She looks at Milton. "You're a pretty awesome dude, too, Mr. Bernstein."

Hal says, "See you guys tomorrow."

Peggy walks them to the front door. As she opens it, the cameras start flashing and a few reporters start shouting questions.

She closes the door behind them and walks back to the den, shaking her head.

Milton looks up from the computer.

Peggy rolls her eyes. "Your brother's something else."

"He's resilient."

"More like brain dead."

"He's Hal. Whatever his brain is lacking he makes up for with his heart."

Peggy, mimicking Patty. "You must be Mr. Bernstein."

Milton smiles. "Maybe my first groupie."

"Belleville, Illinois? Isn't she a little young to be going across state lines with your brother?"

"Are you referring to the White Slave Traffic Act, Chapter 117 of Title 18 of the United States Code, also known as the Mann Act?"

"I have no idea, Milton."

"If so, the age of consent in Missouri is seventeen. The young lady is clearly older than seventeen. Thus under the Mann Act, as amended in 1978, the trip across state lines must be to engage in prostitution or debauchery."

Peggy shook her head in amusement. "Debauchery?"

"That is the term."

"How do you know this?"

"My criminal law professor covered that in class."

"And you still remember it?"

Milton shrugged.

"You're amazing."

"I wish. In any event, tonight's trip to the East Side will not violate the Mann Act. And if it does, this time my brother will be on his own."

Peggy raised her eyebrows. "Debauchery, eh?"

Milton frowned. "Yes?"

"That's an immoral purpose?"

"Under the statute, yes."

She smiled. "I have an idea?"

"Oh?"

"How about transporting me upstairs for some immoral purposes?"

Milton smiles, closes his laptop, and stands. "My pleasure, Mrs. Bernstein."

To see more Poisoned Pen Press titles:

Visit our website:
poisonedpenpress.com/
Request a digital catalog:
info@poisonedpenpress.com